THE LASCAUX PRIZE 2016

THE
LASCAUX PRIZE
2016

edited by
Camille Griep
Stephen Parrish
Wendy Russ

ISBN 10: 0-9851666-5-7
ISBN 13: 978-0-9851666-5-6

Cover design by Wendy Russ.
Cover art by Thomas Cole: "The Oxbow," oil on canvas, 1836.

Lascaux Books
www.lascauxbooks.com

Contents

continued next page

Introduction

Welcome to the third edition of *The Lascaux Prize Anthology* and the first to include flash fiction. Eighteen flash pieces appear in this volume, all entrants in our annual contest. Following these are thirteen poems and eleven longer stories, each culled from thousands of submissions. We trust there is some writing here you will enjoy.

It takes a certain amount of courage to enter a literary contest. Unlike regular submissions, which all too often get buried in a slush pile and are read by bleary-eyed editors, contest entries face a panel of judges. Old world inquisitors. The hounds and gumshoes of the writing industry, who stroke their chins, put entries under magnifying glasses, and squint.

We did quite a lot of chin stroking as we read the entries. And quite a lot of debating, and agonizing. We think writers who have the moxie to enter a literary contest have earned careful scrutiny, and deserve a place under our magnifying glasses. We happen to think they look pretty good there, too.

Our purpose in this volume has been the same as in the others, the same as every editor's: to discover quality writing, to acknowledge it, to bring it to light.

Camille Griep
Stephen Parrish
Wendy Russ

Dragging Raven Lake

by Kevin A. Couture

—for *Lance*

The men waited on the shore while Susan, (whose son they searched for), made coffee on the tailgate of a half-ton. Coffee as black and bitter as the raven scuttling on a branch above them; as black and bitter as the clothes Susan wore, though everyone agreed that was unintentional.

The men took small sips as the boats crept back and forth in prearranged grids. And the raven scrutinized while they adjusted themselves and buttoned their plaid vests against the wind. Their thermos bottles full of the muddy stuff.

More coffee? Susan said and everyone accepted though their hands by this time were shaking and their stomachs burned with acid. Sure, they answered, wiping the muck from their fingers while Susan (who had yet to break down even though this was her only child), poured.

When the boats came in, the men put down their mugs and took hold of the lines. Everyone heaved, hand over hand, wondering if the net seemed heavier this time or were they just getting tired? No, it *was* heavier and the men knew it and Susan knew it by the glances they gave.

And the raven, (who'd maybe had enough or maybe knew more than the men knew), dove from his branch and knocked the pot from Susan's hands. Everyone froze for a moment and stared at the bird screaming on the shore. They stared too at Susan, down on her knees in the sand. Silently scooping up the dregs.

"Dragging Raven Lake" originally appeared in *The Antigonish Review.*

How Did It End?

by Allison Adair

She'd complained about the wind riffling her pages, other cars had air conditioning and out the window in a flash flew the book, our father nimble with generations of training. That arc, that aim, that hand had seen much worse. No one moved though we weren't surprised. The book flapped like a just-broken bird, stranded in its instinct to suspend. The white cover—something about time, a boy, a magnifying glass—hung in the fourth-dimensional pivot between fast with us and still in the grass. Things rarely end where they begin, you know? And with the fields low as they were we could have tucked our skirts and recovered the book one two three along the highway. But the car's red needle was not one to second-guess.

After Mass our father drove north then south again. Our mother looked ahead as he bent near a wire fence, its thin lines hovering like heat upon heat. In the field beyond, a ram bobbed its head under the weight of coiled horns. We rode home, the book between us on the hot vinyl seat. By then a heavy wind had made its way into the spine, swelling our pages with another story.

Shades

by Loren Bienvenu

The foreman wipes down his hands with a rag soaked in lacquer thinner. He should be loading the truck while his crew finishes tearing the rosin paper up from the floor of the house. But it feels nice to stand outside in the late afternoon warmth, breathing air unfiltered by the clammy respirator that was affixed to his face all day. He inhales and exhales. Soon the other two come outside in jumpsuits quilted a hundred different colors, identical to his own except for the randomness of the pattern. He asks them to finish putting the gear back in the truck while he does the final inspection.

In the vacant house, his practiced eye traverses the walls and ceilings. The ground level is spotless. No human signatures to mark his crew's passage—other than the inverse one of newly blanched surfaces. Erasure. Something that indicates itself by virtue of its absence. Ascending the stairs, he envisions a family of strange faces lining the passage. People made life in this dwelling, and more will do so in the future, equally ignorant of predecessor and successor. Ignorant of him, the purgatorial steward shuffling in between. Upstairs are two small bedrooms. The second contains a double mattress wrapped in plastic. He looks out the window of this room and sees his men sitting on the tailgate of the truck below, laughing. Waiting for his return so they can go home where their lovers await. They are hardly more than boys.

The thought grieves him and he turns away. He finds himself sitting on the edge of the mattress. He slowly lowers his body flat amidst the crinkling protest of the covering, then stares upward until his eyelids become heavy.

She used to lie with her head in his lap and gaze at their dappled bedroom ceiling. Identifying beasts in the swirls of white cumulous. *We will create galaxies together*, she once said, both hands on her belly. Tenderly. Soon after she came home with a package of adhesive glow stars and hung them in the sky above their bed. He remembers finding her standing on the bedframe, straining upward with the final star in her hand, endowed with the full potency of myth-making. Establishing with her constellation an origin story from which their ancestors could one day draw derivation.

He sees all of this in the gloaming of his mind. The stars of memory blur and fade, like those on the bedroom ceiling when he swept over them with a loaded paint roller. Trying to erase an absence.

All is quiet. Gone are the eager shouts of the boys lingering out of sight. He begins to drift away. His own bedroom is as blank and vacant as this one, but it offers neither rest nor peace. Soon he is in a deep sleep. For the first time in months. For the first time since his private universe contracted and collapsed, as universes inevitably do.

The Best

by Amy Bonnaffons

The best sex is the sex you never have. So you said, once, perhaps paraphrasing Lacan, and I agreed with you, out loud, although I was not sure if I really meant it, or if you did, either. I did not ask. We were sitting across a low table in a loud bar near the college where we had both recently been hired as lecturers. I said I was tired, though I was not, and you walked me home, though you lived in the opposite direction. When we said goodnight on the sidewalk outside my door, you did not kiss me. You did not take my hand. You did not ask to come upstairs. Maybe because you did not want to do these things, or maybe because you did.

In the following weeks and months and years, we continued not touching each other. We went on dates with other people. We fucked and were fucked by these people. Eventually, we married other people. We created other people with these people. Our lives were peopled by these people we had chosen and created.

During this time, there were so many things you and I did not do. We did not meet each other in crisp-sheeted hotels and solemnly, or wantonly, undress. We did not play hooky from our office hours and slide, in the lazy middle of the day, into the beds warmed and rumpled by our other people, as if sliding into each other's dreams. I did not learn your particular salty smell; we never discovered how well your hand fit or did not fit the curve of my waist, how well we could or could not have worked as interlocking spoons. We were not swept away by any kind of current, because we never even dipped our toes into the current, or got close enough to discover whether there was actually a current at all, or just that occasional, faraway rushing sound, which might have been the wind.

Eventually we left our other people, sick of boredom or of eventfulness, weary of promises broken or too flawlessly fulfilled. Our children rejected us, moved out, accepted us again. We took up hobbies, like gardening, like the restoration of antique motorcycles, like sitting in comfortable chairs and succumbing to distraction. We got re-married or didn't. We regretted, or did not regret, our choices.

During this time, you and I continued not doing things. You did not betray me and I did not betray you. We did not speak ill of the people who had left or re-entered our beds. I did not tell you the strange dreams I forgot as soon as I woke up. You did not show up at my door to stake a claim on the promise that had never been made. We never stopped not loving each other. We never ceased having the conversation we had never begun.

One day we met in the supermarket and as we talked of nothing in particular, leaning against our carts, you touched my hand, by accident or not by accident, and because of that or not because of that, our conversation abruptly ended and we turned away, denying the presence or absence of something that was or was not there, running toward or away from our real lives.

When I got home, I sat in my comfortable chair and stared out the window until it grew dark. I stayed perfectly still. I held both hands in my lap, unmoving, until I lost track of my body completely, until I could no longer remember which one of my hands you had not touched.

Enablers

by Christie Chapman

I swear the conversation starts out intellectual but regresses to "I really want to write a story about a character named Shamalama Dingdong, just because, you know, to do it."

Vince and I meet in bars. If one of us were to ever suggest meeting for coffee, or for food at a place that doesn't serve alcohol, the other one of us would laugh, because that would obviously be a joke. ("Let's meet at McDonald's." "You better mean the one in Germany that has beer.")

I first met Vince at a nightclub. We were both a couple of cocktails into the night, not counting pre-gaming.

He was wearing a sky-blue cowboy shirt that looked like it was made out of felt. He had sideburns, too, like a dirty-blonde Elvis.

Sure enough, he later told me, he'd once placed third in an Elvis-impersonator contest that he'd entered on a lark. The guy who won was a professional Elvis impersonator, and the guy who came in second was a midget, so Vince didn't feel bad about coming in third. "I mean, come on. Midget Elvis."

Vince writes plays, and I write stories.

I tell Vince all the cinematic highlights from my life, and he envisions each one as a scene in a play. His favorite so far was the one of me in the hotel room in New Orleans, clock radio tuned to classic rock, using an exposed pipe as a stripper pole to perform for a guy who was in the room. I was drunk for the first time and had just lost my virginity to a 51-year-old English professor, but none of that real-life backstory or its implications matter that much to Vince— it's the scene in the little room that he likes.

Vince tells me anecdotes from his life—like how he and his mom were homeless for a while, or how he somehow despite being a slacker got into a very good college in Dublin and lived over there for a while and got involved in theater, or how everyone always thinks he's gay but he's not— that make me want to write him up as a character in one of my stories.

Mostly Vince and I talk about writing, a.k.a. life's holiest calling.

"I want to write a story called 'All the Sluts I Knew in High School Now Have Babies and Love Jesus (and All the Nerds I Knew Are Now Sluts).' I've only gotten as far as the title." That one's mine.

Vince and I think of ourselves as the real deal even though neither of us is published. The drinking is an important part of this. We flatter and console ourselves with references to Bukowski and his whiskey. We think of our blighted livers as the hallmarks of suffering saints, like people with stigmata who can feel Jesus's pain so acutely that they bleed where the nails went in.

We like to think of ourselves as bohemian and transgressive, more enlightened and sympathetic to nuance than all the bourgeois people at the "Just Say No" assembly with some guy in a McGruff the Crime Dog costume. Deep down I think we both know that's bullshit, though, and that the nerds at the assembly are right. But Vince and I have trouble with the "just" part of "just say no." We say, "Just one more ... just one more ..."

At some point the talk turns darker. We find relief in mutual confession. "Drunk driving's not so bad. Or I mean, I'm not so bad at it." "Yeah! I'm a pro. I could be in the Drunk-Driving Olympics. I would be on the Drunk-Driving Dream Team." We agree that "The Drunk-Driving Dream Team" would be our name if we ever joined a bowling league or needed a team name for any other reason.

I swear the conversation starts out intellectual but somehow devolves into this.

I tell him about the times I've driven drunk in the middle of the night past the Capitol building, imperious ivory monument to lawfulness. There's this one stoplight that always turns red when I get close to that damn building, and it always feels like it turns red on purpose. As if the universe is forcing me to stop and think about what I'm doing.

"Oh wow. What's going through your mind when that happens?" Vince is the only person I know who asks things like that. He likes to think about a character's "motivation." Both of us are always doing research.

I tell him that I stop and wait for the light to change. I take a swig from the bottle. I look at the white building against the black sky, the unambiguous contrast. I take some more swigs. Then the universe sighs in exasperation, as if thinking, "You are not taking this seriously." Then the light turns green and it lets me go.

"You didn't really answer my question."

"Yes I did."

"I want to write a love story that's just a bunch of drunk text messages."

There was one time that Vince and I hung out sober. It was early on before we knew better. We sat in a bagel place and asked each other about our jobs. I was painfully aware of everything around us. He shook a sugar packet and ripped off the top before pouring it into his coffee. Our capers didn't stick to the cream cheese and kept rolling onto the table. I strained for something deep to say. There were families with kids everywhere, a pestilence of children. The sun through the window was bright on our faces and made us look old. We vowed to never do it again.

I tell Vince about my dad's cousin who died of cirrhosis. She was always drunk. My dad said this about her: "I never saw Gail when she wasn't happy."

We raise a toast to Gail. Vince says, "May the same be said of us someday." We clink glasses and drink.

Heaven Spoils
by Gay Degani

Black clouds dome the sky, the color blue forgotten. Rain drowns tomatoes and strips the fig tree outside my window. And it's kept on for weeks, those fat drops hammering the roof. Inside, Mother reads about Noah. She watches for arks.

Father dies, then Danny dies. Maybe the pox, we don't know for sure. No neighbors on our lonely road. No doctor for a hundred miles. We wrap them both in potato sacks, and drag them through the storm and into the shed; whisper prayers, lock the door. Water and sludge make digging graves impossible.

The house has become a dank basement. Water seeps through seams, warps wood, turns flour to paste. The cold is everywhere, in the bed sheets, in my underwear. Clothes cling to skin. Hair clings to scalp. We burn the kitchen chairs for warmth.

Mother sends me to the chicken coop. The mud in the yard, deep and heavy and thick, sucks off my shoes, so I fall to my knees and crawl. The stench inside is wrenching. I find no eggs and one quivering hen in the corner.

After the bird is eaten, the candles burned, I tell her we have to go. She doesn't look up from her psalms. I pack our things. Help her with her oil-skin slicker.

We take the Bible, some tattered dollar bills, the re-maining cans of tuna and beans and the last of our water, a tent, and two umbrellas. Mother grips my arm as we slog along. I wish I could read the mud the same way people from the north read the snow.

The umbrellas snap and the tent begins to tear. Mother dies on the fifth night. I curse her for taking the easy way out and kick around in the sludge, pulling my hair. Then cursing myself, I drop to the soggy ground and beg for her forgiveness. I curl beside her, head tucked into her shoul-der, rain pelting down, like dirt on a grave.

Mother's in the kitchen with a wooden mallet in her hand, tenderizing the shanks of our cow, sun slanting through the kitchen window, birds outside pecking at figs, Father in the field, and Danny fixing the wire on the chick-en coop. I am not there.

When I wake, I wipe the muck from Mother's face and crossing her arms, tuck the Bible underneath, cover her with branches from dying trees, and trudge on.

I squint at the invisible road ahead, rain drumming down, my constant companion, mud disappearing under rising water, my shoes like paper, my toes and fingers numb. Raindrops burn my eyes. I listen for the drone of planes; watch for car lights flashing in the distance. I am all that is left of those I know. I keep an eye out for any kind of ark.

"Heaven Spoils" originally appeared in *Rattle of Want* (Pure Slush Press).

Quakes

by Ryann Eastman

As a child, I packed a natural disaster bag every night. My favorite sweatshirt, a picnic blanket, a pair of sneakers with thick socks. My stuffed tiger, a copy of the third Harry Potter, and a letter from the tooth fairy. I'd go over the exit routes before bed. Check the door for a fire; take the back if the knob is hot. If the ground starts to shake, roll off the bed and under it. I imagined having super speed, being fast enough to shoot upstairs, scoop up my cat before the ceiling could split. Every night, I lay in bed and thought of standing on the lawn in bare feet, hugging my emergency pack. Waiting for my parents to emerge from the front door.

*

My mother, seven-months pregnant and driving a red Honda sedan with a cracked fender, was halfway across the bridge when the Loma Prieta Earthquake smashed into the Bay Area. She was three hundred feet from the mouth of Treasure Island and going seventy-five when the bridge shifted. The car shuddered on cement, lurching to the guardrail and, first thing, she grabbed her stomach with one hand and thought, *if I drive into that tunnel, it's going to collapse.* The whole island will tumble down and I'll drown in the estuary. My husband will watch my obituary on the television, as a reporter relays the information that—oh god, the victim was pregnant. Another soul lost to that California curse.

She braked, skidded sideways across two lanes. But the reinforcements kept and the bridge didn't fall. A section of the upper deck had buckled behind her and, with her only route home blocked; she drove into the city, thanking God that she'd filled the gas tank that morning, not brave enough to stop for a payphone.

My father, who knew she was going to San Francisco that day, stayed next to the phone, searched the news channels. Across town, the cement slab of the Nimitz overpass had collapsed, flattening the freeway below, a line of cars crushed like soda cans. My mother called him three hours later, from a payphone at the Ritz-Carlton. "The family called, no one was hurt," he told her. My mother, who had never lived anywhere other than California, leaned against the wallpapered side of the payphone cubicle and nodded.

Growing up, they teach us how to handle it. Get under a sturdy table or a bed. Crouch behind the back of your sofa. Stand in a doorjamb and close your eyes. There'll be no warning, or news stories, or email alerts. It has to be instinct—take cover, get out of the house, don't go back, and don't try to save anyone.

My mother made jokes about her pregnancy; called me an earthquake baby. Told her friends, laughing, "That daughter of mine is a *real* California girl."

*

"You're a strong willed woman. If you think about something enough, it may come true," my mother always told me, and I believed her. As I considered my exit plan, laying in my twin bed on black and orange Lion King sheets, I felt like I was inviting the earthquake. As if I was personally responsible for the shifting ground, the boiling basalt, the San Andreas Fault. One night, certain I was conjuring a disaster—not natural anymore, but mine—I snuck outside. This close to the city, you could only spot a few stars in the sky, little dots and, every now and then, the travelling blink of a plane. I sat on the wet grass; dew soaking through my flannel pajama bottoms, and imagined a dome around my house. A transparent safety dome, starting high up in the air and cascading down, covering the lawn and the pool, my mother's Zen garden and the stone fountain, the two story house and all of the nice, pretty things inside. My calico cat and my two parents—all secure within a force field. A fire could burn by and be deflected, just an arced plume of orange; a flood would be dammed at the edge of the property, sloshing and rising up the curved field. And the dome went under the ground too, locking together the plates of the earth. I stayed there all night, knees pulled to my chest, waiting for the shimmering film to appear.

Well Built Men, 18 to 30, Who Would Like to Be Eaten by Me

by Jen Fawkes

You find it in Tristan's room, an ad excised from the personals, folded in even thirds, tucked into a collection of South American folktales. The book was a gift from Tristan's first boss, the *Capitan* of a Bolivian crew that once cleaned his father's law office. Tristan was nineteen then, the youngest of four boys, a rising college sophomore home for summer break, and you thought the janitorial job beneath him. But when you pointed this out to Dean, who'd not yet left you for his twenty-three-year-old paralegal, who'd not yet discovered that, within the walls of his colon, a malignant mass was marshalling its fatal forces, your then-husband seized your slight shoulders. *You've got to face facts, Connie,* he said. *The boy's never been right.* It was true that Tristan was always unnaturally attached, that unlike his brothers, who tore themselves from the temple of your flesh early on, who blazed trails toward wives, children, careers in periodontal care and hunger relief, Tristan

19

always clung to you. Hid in your shadows. He was the only one to show interest in your former life as a human oddity, a contortionist known, on the southeastern carnival circuit, as Collapsible Connie. Your specialty was dislocating your shoulders, folding your limbs, knitting your bones into an impossible rectangle of humanity, one small enough to stuff inside a lock-box. You learned the secrets of escaping such a prison from your uncle Mesmer, a tiny man who sprang from the heart of the Bolivian rainforest, spawned by the chieftain of a purportedly anthropophagus tribe. When you were twelve, Mesmer was devoured by a docile lion named Daphne, and for years afterward, when no one was looking, you would sneak off to Daphne's cage, pry open her colossal jaws, lay your head against the rough pillow of her tongue. *Go on*, you would whisper, *take me, too*. But you received, in response, only a humming purr. Tristan was the only person to whom you revealed this, the only person to whom you admitted that, at zoos, you never stopped jealously eyeing the raw meat fed to big cats. From the moment you first held your youngest, you understood that he inherited your flexibility, and you taught him everything you know about contortion, about compliance. Seven years after Tristan received his BA in Anthropology, Dean was consumed by cancer, and since your ex-husband never got around to marrying his poor paralegal, his money went to your sons. You and Tristan pooled your resources and, on the twenty-eighth anniversary of his birth, put down a deposit on this Craftsman bungalow. Three days ago, your son departed for an overnight camping trip, and still, he hasn't returned. When you invade the sanctity of his room, you discover the personal ad, and your eyes feast on the unnatural words. You think of Shirley Loomis, who once informed you that, while spending the night at her house, your ten-year-old son begged her boy Jimmy to eat him. *Please,* Tristan said. *Swallow my flesh.* You never mentioned this to Dean; even you and Tristan never discussed your shared desire to be ingested, to escape this mortal cage via esophagus, stomach, intestines. And now, rather than calling the police, you find yourself collapsing, folding your limbs, knitting up your bones. You cower on the carpet, the slightest version of yourself, wondering when Tristan emerged from your shadows. At what point you crawled into his.

"Well Built Men, 18 to 30, Who Would Like to Be Eaten by Me" originally appeared in *Blue Earth Review.*

Lazy Lies

by Robin Hunter

I had the abortion on Monday and he already wants me to go back to work. Someone will have to pay the overdue Internet bill before he's cut off from a world of online correspondence schools and anime pornography. I don't bother arguing the merits of either. I get exhausted just thinking about the fight we would have and continually opt to keep my mouth shut. We both seem to prefer it that way.

When we met he was a painter selling prints at art shows and I was a writer selling nothing, nowhere. The conversations were long and varied, as was the sex, but soon the relationship morphed from tantalizing to tiresome and I was continually the one to blame.

The night we conceived he had failed an open-book test for his Dystopian Literature class and I had no choice but to quiet his rails against George Orwell with lazy kissing and unshaven nakedness, my bare hip tattooed in pen transfer from poorly scribbled notes on *1984*.

Now, I know it was a bad idea, getting ready for my first day back at work, squeezing my bloated form into a pencil skirt, fastening it with a rusted safety pin. My shaky hand slips and I prick my finger, feeling nothing.

"You look beautiful," he tells me and I know he is lying. When I leave the house he will jerk off in front of the computer and fall asleep on the couch. "Can you bring home dinner? I'm thinking Chinese."

Sitting at my desk, during the mid-afternoon lull, I think I feel the baby kick and jump from my seat to tell my cubicle-mate Dan. I want him to put his hand to my belly, to tell me I am not crazy, but he's in a meeting and I am crazy. It's all in my mind, the kicking, the swelling, the feeling of being a twosome, rather than a one-some with a boy-friend.

On our one-year anniversary I took a pregnancy test, believing a wine-fueled night, at his grandparents' cottage, had led to the biggest mistake of our lives. He held my hand for three minutes, telling me everything would be okay, that he would take care of *us*. For a moment, I loved him. When the test developed negative lines I was saddened we couldn't stay that way forever, trapped in three-minute intervals of comfort and connectivity. That night, he went out with friends to celebrate the "good news." I should have left him then, but the apartment is rent controlled.

When it happened again two years later, he didn't wait for the results, he was already out drinking.

Dan returns, bleary-eyed from Power Point, but still able to map the curve of my ass as I lean over my desk. I do it on purpose, knowing he likes to look, but today, bent forward and feeling sick, I suddenly vomit my breakfast, stopping short of letting it leak from my mouth. Rushing to the cramped bathroom, maple spiced oatmeal quickly fills the bowl as sweat pools on my back, soaking my blouse.

"Are you alright?" Dan asks, his shined shoes poking into the stall. "It sounds like you still have that bug."

No. I don't have that bug anymore.

Let's Not Move to Poland

by David Karosick

He's absolutely convinced the Holocaust happened in this house.

The Holocaust did not happen in this house.

I don't want to live here.

I tell him the Holocaust happened in lots of places a long time ago and that it didn't happen here. I tell him to google it. It's vola-nee-met-schka but with a W not a V. Yesterday he googled cynodon dactylon because it sounds like a flying dinosaur.

The road is mostly dirt, a woman with knapsack-brown skin wheelbarrows by, I lean into my shoulders. He types next to me. I watch his serious eyes go wide until they're panoramic. He holds out his phone. W-O-L-A and google suggests wola massacre and suddenly his screen is lit in black and red.

I stand. I brush off the dirt.

What if he finds out that slaughter is the way it goes here. That this place is combustible or at least that history has shown the conditions right for combustion. That this climate bends toward frenzy. That the fossil record confirms centuries of destabilization. That its borders are mealy. That of the dynasty of national powder kegs, it is a founding member. Every vine is an unlit fuse, gunpowder laces the soil, the trees are centrifuges disguised as trees.

I take his phone and type.

See, I say, that was a different Wola.

I don't want to live here, he says.

Look at that funny little woman with the wheelbarrow.

Ohio Grass

by Scott Kauffman

You never consider how it will end when it begins. Certainly you never considered how on the night you met;
that date horn-dog Dave set you up on where you sat waiting on a stool, telling yourself to stop looking at your watch
and looking every fifteen seconds anyway. As the gray-
haired bartender poured you your third shooter of Old
Granddad, a hand touched your shoulder. She spoke your
name with a question mark hung on the end, and you swiv-
eled around, forever lost in eyes as green as a sea of Ohio
grass. You never considered how it would end as she sat
beside you, her dark visage mirrored in the tulip-poplar
wood but considered only how you might jive her number
before she finished her *pina colada* and disappeared again
into the rain. As she crossed to the door, you sat at the bar
considering the sway of her hips, her chartreuse-print dress
through the plate-glass window running like a *Monet*. You

left to consider the number she wrote in her calligraphic script across your wrist, her fingertips touching your veins as if she might divine what to be true in your heart. You never considered how it would end two dates later when she let you kiss her, her breath fresh as linen sheets whipping in April sunshine. You never considered how it would end when the two of you laid on a blanket in the just-cut hayfield behind the house where she grew up, her mother calling and calling from the back porch, the screen door slamming, and the next morning she refused to speak to either of you except to ask how you wanted your eggs. You never considered how it would end as the two of you stood in her country church that rose out of a sea of Ohio grass, the hand with which she had written on your wrist in her calligraphic script now a vice gripping yours as she vowed until death do you part, her other at her side with no need to touch the veins pulsing your wrist. You never considered how it would end until you ceased the mouth-to-mouth you started after you called 911. Your heart hammered as you forced your first breath into her breast, praying it was hers that respired in answer but knew it to be the echo of your own. You stand and unlock the front door and return to wait beside her where she lies in a pool of fecaled blood, her milky skin curdled orange. Her eyes open to the first sight of what is or is not. Her mouth ajar. Words she wanted to say but had not the breath? Or had the breath, but you were not with her to hear. You will see her once more when you bequeath her beneath a sea of Ohio grass, but those green eyes will forever be sewn shut. Running boots pound up the porch steps. The four men who enter put an end to your prayers. They speak words you are not ready to hear and bodybag her away, you left to consider how in the pool of fecaled blood the imprint of her hand with which she had written on your wrist in her calligraphic script darkens in the crepuscular light.

Brizls

by Scott Lambridis

All Brizls should be put out of their misery and shot. I hate Brizls. Who would ever want to be a Brizl? Who could ever love a Brizl? They're all the same.

At birth, they are hollow and lumpy, unformed only because they are not yet malformed, and yet when they learn to speak, they'll say, "Can I be a lion," or "Can I be a spider," or "Can I be a raindrop. Can I at least be a raindrop?" Of course not.

In life, they are a burden to those around them—*such* a burden!—and when, on occasion, they overcome this sense of burdening through honorable acts, a favor here, a warm meal there, maybe an extra trip to the meat counter, maybe a handwritten card, or a romantic evening though they are worthless lovers, maybe even a late-night conversation though they'd rather be sleeping, then they feel the burden of others upon themselves—oh, such a *burden!*—that they become solitary again and mourn their birth until someone, usually another Brizl, talks them out of it.

When dirty, they wash their hands. When stubborn, they lean back into a large and deep seat, placing their arms firmly on the arm rests. And yet they poison their bodies to escape the creeping eclipse of time. People bend around them as if they were demons, barely there, but there, only there. You can see that their own voices make them cringe, though they deny it when asked. Once, on a train, in the glossy reflection of a window, I saw a Brizl shave his face, and I wasn't surprised. They can simultaneously condemn their own hateful natures, and yet while exiting that same train and seeing a child wandering toward a blind man's stick, *tap-tap*, *tap-tap*, a Brizl will indulge in his own desire for them to collide, just to see what happens, and yet they are not considered unstable?

They're even given respectable jobs. And everyone in the consulting world knows those moments when, during a meeting, the facilitator reads off the roll, and you know, just by their last names, and the look on their faces, that they are all Brizls, and embarrassed, one of them leaves, and then another, until you cannot even have your meeting anymore. All decisions are off, until two months later, you find a new set of consultants and it happens again. Their companies are crippled and make no money. It is right that they should be feared. They understand nothing.

But in death, they are the worst. When they choose to die, which is often early, when they hit that age that is the age that can be tolerated no longer, they feel that uncontrollable desire to orchestrate their own deaths, and they announce it, fourteen days in advance, inviting murder, in their shrill voices that the animals cannot even hear, and they don't simply crawl inside themselves, or burrow into the ground. They ask others, usually another Brizl, to help them die, burdening their families and friends, Brizl or otherwise (though none but a Brizl could be their friend, or could love one enough to become family). May I use your house? The spare bedroom would be perfect. I'll be quiet. You won't even know I'm there. I'll pay the extra utilities in advance. And when they are asked, out of courtesy, what is troubling them, why can't they just suck it up like everyone else, they say something that sounds like the usual feelings everyone can understand, but they lie. The real emotion is inside still, unsaid. "You'll never really understand. You're not a Brizl," As if that's any real sort of excuse.

And then, at last, what's truly worst of all of them, is the extremity of self-loathing practiced by each and every Brizl like an art form passed down generation after generation, which unfolds like devil wings as they write letters of apology and tack them to their wasted bodies, puncturing it, opening a hole for that slow leak they know others will see, staining whatever vessel they collapse into.

And then there they are, today, in a plastic blow-up pool on the front lawn, so that someone will see, someone will be bothered with the cleanup, as if those fluids are something to mourn. And they will each of them leave behind only a long list of failures, memorials to their own ineptitude and inability to evolve, so that their children—sad for just that initial moment—are then filled with the inspiration that they too can do the world a world of good and reduce the burden they have placed upon it.

No, I hate them, and I do not want to be a Brizl anymore.

I Shouldn't Send This
by Cassidy McCants

25 November 2011

I'm writing you because I was reminded of you yesterday the same way I sometimes remember snow exists when I'm sweating in the Dallas heat.

Do you remember when I sent you that poem about Thanksgiving a few years back? About how my mom would always have a nervous breakdown at family gatherings? I just wished you'd come for the holidays with me. I almost slapped her as I sat watching her take drink after drink after drink. But instead, from the guestroom window, I watched the first snow fall, wrote a poem and sent it to you.

You never responded.

Yesterday, I found myself pouring a fifth, maybe sixth—something like that—gin and tonic. It was a little after one, just before the sweet potatoes were ready. And you know what I realized? Maybe I couldn't eat dinner with everyone. Maybe I'd just work on this last drink, nibble on a roll and watch as everyone decided between pumpkin and apple pie. It was still early in the day; I could eat later, whenever I got hungry. There are always leftovers.

I never got hungry.

Do you remember when I returned from Little Rock that year? We sat in the kitchen playing Strip Scrabble as I finished up a bottle of wine and you drank your gin. You and that gin. Then we moved on the bed by the light of the fiber-optic Christmas tree and the flame of a cinnamon-scented candle.

Now I'm suddenly aware that I will never see the muscles in your back moving like that again. That I don't have you to share these thoughts with. Unless, of course, I actually send this letter.

Maybe I didn't mean to leave you alone with your guitar in Nashville that winter. Maybe you were right in believing that we could make everything work. But how could I have believed in promises so perfect? Do you know what I'm saying? Things never don't fall apart, if you think in double negatives. I do lately. Things always fall apart. Everything melts. Everything fades. Everything changes. But what I'm saying is that maybe I could have at least given things a chance.

I still use words like "things." All the time. Now, I know that maybe there's nothing smart in being subtle, but I'm still never completely comfortable with specificity. I know you always hated that.

If I send this letter, I might never hear back from you.

This year, I find it hard to blame my mother. Remember the opening line of that poem? "I always wonder if Grandma did this too," I believe. Was I really wondering if Grandma did it too? Maybe I was just wondering if one day *I'd* be the one without an appetite. If I'd be the one saying that it'd just been a stressful week at work. If I'd ever have that sadness in my voice—the permanent kind—the kind that's present in someone's voice regardless of what's going on.

You know she let my father go? She let the one man who loved her go because she wasn't willing to be that vulnerable. I told myself I would never do the same.

I had a dream a few weeks ago about a train. A man in a pick-up was in front of me on the road, waiting beside the tracks of a passing train. I guess his truck inched forward a bit, and suddenly the train was destroying the hood of the vehicle. More and more of the front kept disappearing. I hopped out of my car (I assume I was in a car; I don't remember actually being in one) and opened the man's door. He sat there in shock, and I yelled at him to get out. He finally jumped out of his seat onto the street just before the train took the cab of the truck. His eyes were extremely wide and extremely blue, and he said to me, "You saved me." That's all he said, and that's all I wanted to hear.

You always said I saved you. And then I left. Are you unsaved now? How does that work?

Last night, my mom asked about you. She asked if you still send me songs.

I told her yes, because I still sleep every night to the sounds of what I know to be your words, the calming harmonies that are somehow so clearly your essence. There's a chance of snow tomorrow morning. Maybe I'll dream of winter set to your songs, but I know I'll wake up and wish for warmth the second I step outside.

There are always leftovers.

Like Snowflakes

by Neleigh Olson

I'm alone in Denver. And you know what? Good. Good. I don't even care that it's snowing. I like the snow. Love it. I'd love to pull the sky down on the city, tuck inside, and wrap myself up in all that coldness.

The suitcase is propped against an orange settee his mother gave us as an engagement gift. Should the sky actually fall and cover us in snow, the settee and its fragile upholstery would be unsalvageable. The suitcase is a softcover roller case, blue, with one bad wheel, and got lost in Houston on its way home. It doesn't realize this, but it is still lost. It is across the room from me, three years, two days and a trip to Costa Rica between us. It is not my suitcase. It's f'ing Steve's suitcase.

The tag on the bag says "Walters," and that's how this happened. The name on the marriage certificate says "Walters," the name on our mailbox says "Walters" and I when I sign my name, I learned to curl the tips of the "W" when I write "Walters." The other Walters is home in North Hollywood with the bag whose W's have curly points, and his bag is here with me in our very empty Denver condo. I got all A's in high school Spanish, but I suppose some things fall away with the years. They're not supposed to, but they do. That's how people end up with misplaced suitcases. There is no chapter in a high school Spanish book that tells a person how to change a return flight, how to kiss your husband through the taste of her lips on his, how to turn away and not look back.

What I should do is open the damn thing. I should open it and pull out every piece of him, scatter it on the floor, breathe in the scent of it. I'd unzip the pockets and there would be the touch of his hand, warm on the small of my back. A thousand secret jokes and midnight conversations would fall onto the condo's carpet, and the more we tried to stop laughing the more we couldn't, because we knew the neighbors would start pounding on the wall again. I'd search and search and when I was happy with the mess, I'd fold up the pieces and tuck them back inside.

I've read that if you drop a penny off the top of the Empire State Building, the force if it's velocity would be enough to kill a person standing below who doesn't know to be watching out for things that could fall out nowhere.

The outline of his vacation sandals reach out to me from the front pocket. When I pull them out, they drop grains of sand across the carpet, and this makes me so angry I nearly cry. Because you don't do that to a person. Because I'd told him that the sand was hot and that it would burn his feet. Scald him. But the sandals are here, still warm and horrible and making a mess on such a nice floor.

The suitcase is heavier than it looks, and the weight of it surprises me. A thick frosting of snow covers the porch and softens the edges on all of the benches and trees in the courtyard below. A gray sky sprinkles down around me. I welcome its coldness into my lungs and feel it pour through my body. The suitcase looks dangerous, suicidal, beautiful perched on the railing. When I go through with it, the suitcase explodes. Look out below! A flurry of t-shirts, shorts, plastic baggies and travel-sized bottles fall beyond my outstretched fingers. Mixed with the cold and the snow and that gray sky, I watch Costa Rica fall into my courtyard, with the warmth of his sandals still on my palms.

The Hardship of the
Insufficiently Afflicted

by Melissa Ostrom

Doctor Sherwin Peterson left Carissa for Faith, a former patient. Long after an unfortunate diagnosis had forced Faith to seek more specialized medical care, Dr. Peterson, her primary physician, maintained a profound interest in her situation. He admired her for bravely facing and besting breast cancer, all while writing about her fight and raising public awareness, as well as substantial funds for research.

The doctor-patient love story, so heartwarming, blurred the issue of infidelity. Sherwin and Faith's romance, grounded in mutual esteem and fueled by high stakes, the very struggle for life, made the betrayed spouse's outrage unseemly, her frustration and bitterness petty. Even those closest to her hesitated to condemn a cancer survivor and the supportive doctor and suitor.

When Carissa complained she felt as maligned as a malignant tumor, Meg, her best friend, actually winced. "You shouldn't make light of a tumor, Car."

Carissa seethed. *She* was the wronged party. Didn't anyone get that?

The day her impending ex-husband removed certain belongings from their soon-to-be-sold brownstone, recollections, old ones, contributed to her sense of ill-usage. She remembered when her mother had divorced her father, packed two suitcases, and moved to Guatemala to teach at an orphanage. She recalled how her single father, every Christmas after that, had asked her and her sister, Jenny, to each select one of their recently received gifts to donate to a toy drive for poor children. And she thought about the time, a year before her mother left, when she and Jenny had gone sledding and slammed straight into a tree at the bottom of the hill. The impact had bloodied Carissa's nose, but Jenny had suffered a broken arm.

The circumstances, though varied, taught Carissa the same irksome lesson: there was always someone whose troubles warranted greater concern and interest.

Pained distaste tightened the husband's expression on his last visit, as he went from room to room with funereal calm, collecting a few items, nothing big, that he claimed belonged exclusively to him. Carissa stalked him with heated words, hungry for an argument, heckling and harassing him. He refused to get drawn into a battle over the purple coffee mug, an old book of poems, a little painting. At the least sign of her revving for a skirmish, he relinquished the source of contention with an austere nod, as if to demonstrate his maturity, how he was above such trifling tiffs.

In the office, over the wide, curly maple desk (her wedding present to him, though she'd never let him keep it now, not if he begged, not if she had to throw her body across it to protect it from his two-timing clutches), he asked with icy detachment, "May I at least take my laptop?"

"As soon as I'm done breaking it."

He left shortly after that.

Following, she pushed the office chair out of the room then through the front door, wishing she could shove it quickly enough to hurl it at him before he walked away, wishing she were strong enough to slam it across his smoothly departing Mercedes. She didn't want the chair. She, in fact, refused to sit in it: the seat he'd used to carry on his supportive, tender email exchange with Faith.

A spring broke when she flung it down the stoop steps. Though it landed right side up, the black, cushioned top now tilted. It looked like a head cocked for listening, so she told it, "I hate you."

She kicked it across the sidewalk to the curb then tried to topple it, but instead of falling over, it just kept rolling along the dingy strip of August-burned grass. This forced her to hook a foot on the wheeled bottom, to hold it in place while she strained to flip it, a clumsy wrangling that cost her her balance. When it at last tipped, she did too and landed on top of it.

A young couple, teenagers, slowed their car as they passed, and the girl leaned out the opened window to laugh, "Get a room, lady!"

Panting and limping, Carissa returned to the house, her right ankle sore, maybe even broken, she thought hopefully, calculating how her injured status would impact Sherwin and Faith, how it'd repaint the heroic lovers and their passion-that-knows-no-bounds-fueled adultery.

Carissa pictured herself with one foot, the other having been amputated after the ankle gangrened. She would travel the country with her prosthetic foot and deliver speeches of inspiration and hope to girl scouts and injured veterans and graduating seniors and scorned divorced women. She would raise money for all their causes.

She would make her husband's cruel infidelity one of the obstacles she overcame. Her speech would be a story of tragedy, woe, and triumph. The most moving story. Ever.

Anya

by Karen Smyte

She could feather the blade with a subtle push down of her middle finger on the oarhandle. Loose, liquid. Can't coach something like that. She studied piano, years. A weaver of rugs or surgeon or shooter, in a different life.

This ease allowed her to feel the water and unlock her power early. In rowing, the hands are the first to respond to fear. Anya was sure with her hands. From the start, she suspended all her weight on the oarhandle, unafraid, trusting her fingers to link her to the water, pure connection, as if the oar was an extension of her hands, an appendage she was born with. Natural, some say, but it's the kind of intelligence that unnerves because it's unusual. I ask my women to hang on the blade, backs firm against the leg jump. I share similes, hoping "like a child hanging on monkey bars" will illuminate. I manipulate bodies, show video. Eventually, most learn. A handful are like Anya.

Practice that day five 1500's. The crew, while capable of concentration, distracted easily by other boats or birds alighting close to us. My girls were slow bringing their blades down, sleepwalked to the back of the boathouse bay to take the shell out. I allowed this dreamlike motion, never sure if this was kindness. I claimed not to know the names of their favorite musicians, pretended to be older than I was, closer to their parents. I talked about lifting the hands as they approached the catch so their blades entered at their long point and they could suspend properly. Four weeks Anya had been missing. What else could we do?

"Relax as you come up the slide," I told them when we stopped on the water between intervals, desperate for them to balance their bodies and feel the boat run under them. Only Bridgette released the blade quietly from a dark, tight swirl: the others ripped their blades out, splashing wash up, loudly, like buckets of water thrown on the floor. "You're tearing the water," I told them. "It isn't only about power. It's how you control it." They bloomed the last piece, rowed lighter to the dock. When they put their boat away, their laughter made the boys' team skittish, like dogs on the street waiting on scraps of meat and bones.

After work, I walked through my door and played my messages. "Call me," Sue said. I brought the chimes that hung on my balcony into the living room, directed a small fan on low for a constant wind to push the metal pieces randomly together. The tinkling reminded me of the sound small bits of canal ice make with the spring thaw, when water gently laps and pushes the pieces against the shore and one another. I wanted some kind of auditory cover, but the voices of the children playing baseball in the courtyard of the building, their admonishments and trash talk and hilarity, the crack, crack of the bat, noise. I closed the window. The radio and stereo ridiculous, too, with vocals and melodies and harmonies, attempts at control but none of it would change a thing. The ringing of the chimes I could believe in.

Our fears realized.

We'd hoped Anya was different, unusual in her disappearance. But after days of dredging the canal, divers, policemen more familiar with breaking up fights between best friends at junior hockey games, pulled up Anya's body. One of them had talked with her mother only two days earlier, had slipped into magical thinking despite intimate knowledge of statistics, of Anya's chances this long disappeared. But girls disappear every day.

Bridgette dropped by. She'd been before to watch rowing videos, to talk about her job, to eat and avoid home. "The secretary mispronounced her name in announcements," she told me. I didn't ask how the sounds were twisted. Did the secretary say Anna? Anu? Anneke? Polyanski? "How could she mess it up, coach?" I made tea and put cookies on a plate, having absorbed the rituals I witnessed my mother perform for years. Feed people. I was thankful for Bridgette and her vitality, would have let her stay as long as she wanted, but her mother phoned and called B home.

Her name was Anya Polyanskaya. I loved to watch her row. And her hands. She feathered the blade with a gentle push down of her middle finger on the oarhandle, loose, relaxed. A dentist, a seamstress, a jeweler, in another life.

"Anya" won the 2015 Stella Kupferberg Memorial Short Story Prize and originally appeared in *Electric Literature*.

Our Trip to the Moon
by Bob Thurber

When my brother and I were barely more than babies our grandfather took us to the moon. I don't expect anyone to believe me, and frankly I don't remember how we got there, what we did for air, or how we got back, and neither, sadly, does my brother. This was years ago, right after our mother had died in a horrible accident, so we were still pretty young—my brother barely walking, me just turned three—and at those ages a person's sleep patterns are still pretty crazy, so I'm guessing we snoozed on the ride there and back. If we went in a rocket or some kind of spaceship we probably had padded seats, or comfy little beds with straps to hold us in, but if we got to the moon by a ladder then I guess my grandfather must have carried us, each on a shoulder, like two uneven sacks of grain.

I do remember we were dressed in heavy fur coats with hoods over clinging knitted caps, and that we wore rubber boots and wool mittens, with long, colorful scarves secured around half our faces. And that it was very dark, and very cold. My brother was petrified of the dark and he's still afraid of it now, and though I've never been afraid of anything I didn't like the extreme cold or the strangeness of the place.

"I want to go home," I said boldly.

"We just got here," Grandpa said.

"Trey wants to go too," I said, pointing at my brother, who was clinging to Grandpa's leg like a bear cub stuck up a tree, and whimpering like one too.

"Listen to me," grandpa said. "This is a great place. I used to bring your mother here when she was a little girl. She loved it, and I'll tell you why. Nothing changes here. Not ever. Unlike Earth, there's no erosion. No wind or rain, no storms or volcanic activity to shift what's beneath your feet and change the surface. Nothing ever gets washed away or covered over, or swallowed up. Nothing gets folded back inside itself, then buried and forgotten. Have a quick look around. The footprints made by the first Apollo Astronauts are right over there and they'll remain visible for as long as the moon exists." Then he grinned like that crazy cat in that crazy story. "Your mother's footprints are here too," he said. "See if you can find them."

Then grandpa just let us run loose. We went together, my brother and I, holding hands, and we found our mother's footsteps faster than if we had a map. We placed our feet inside her prints, which weren't much larger than our own. We hopped a few strides, tracing her trail, leaping higher and easier than I expected. Then we got tired of that and just played in the dust like it was snow, stomping around, leaving patterns, making snow angels, kicking up so much moon dust that it floated around us like we were inside a snow globe that someone had given a really hard shake. I imagine he did that. My grandfather. He was always shaking things up.

The Neurotic's Guide to Navigating Breakfast
by Ruth Wyer

There are 183 words on the back of a family-sized box of Kellogg's All Bran. Not enough for your purpose but as you are first to the table, choose it; at thirty centimetres high it offers the best protection. Weet-Bix may well be your preferred start to the day but at only ten centimetres tall it's of no use to you here. Leave it for the latecomers. Your sister, Grace, will appear from the kitchen eight years older than when you last saw her; her jowls melting over her jawbone as though she had stood too long in summer at a west-facing window. She will hand you a spoon and a knife as she sits beside you. Accept them without hesitation and do not check them for the dried remnants of previous meals; germaphobes are a tiresome lot and you don't want to be mistaken for one.

Your brother-in-law, Phil, will lumber down the stairs and throw himself into the chair opposite with such force that he will knock your cutlery out of parallel alignment.

Don't waste energy convincing yourself you can ignore this. Just realign them. Hold the packet directly in front of you. It will not cover nearly as much of Phil as you hope so lean closer to the box and eat with your head lowered. Read the words slowly, forwards at first, then backwards (twice) before grouping them into fives. Groups of threes are more your thing but you can do those in your sleep and you will need a far greater challenge if you are going to make it through the meal.

Notice that the word LIFE is made up of perfectly matched pairs of lines that can be removed two at a time until nothing remains.

There will be far more words and interesting facts on the side of the packet but resist the urge to turn it sideways as Phil will be using his tongue as a tugboat, guiding the spoon of cereal into his mouth as if he does not trust it can make it there under the steam of his arm alone. Try not to think of how you might have stayed in the motel just outside town. It doesn't matter now that, against your better judgment, you had answered the phone and somewhere between Grace's protestations of "We won't hear of it," and "Family is Family," you had accepted her invitation only so that you did not have to listen to the concern in her voice masquerading as false cheer.

Phil will drag reluctant pats of butter screaming across the charred surface of his toast. The sound will cause jagged flashes of pain deep in your skull. There's a real possibility you might use your own knife to skewer Phil's hand to the floral tablecloth, so consider humming a jaunty tune. Exuding a positive air is particularly important as Grace has always been the mothering type and is not above removing your cereal box and insisting that you sit upright and engage with those around you. You will consider this a moment too long and Grace will gently pull the All Bran from your grasp and place it out of reach behind the orange juice. She will say something you will not hear as, with your shield gone, the microwave clock will now be directly in your line of vision. Its four digits line up perfectly with your own fingers compelling you to trace and retrace the numbers against the tabletop (index and pinkie fingers on the vertical lines, middle and ring fingers on the horizontal lines) until a new minute ticks over and the whole process begins again.

Proliferous, these digital clocks. Breeding like nits. Colonising the corners of appliances. Infiltrating every room with their constant itch that must be scratched. When you still had your own home you covered the clocks with Post-it notes and scrawled random tasks on them. "Oh those?" you would say if anyone asked, dismissing them with a casual wave of your hand, "Just little reminders. I'd forget my head if it wasn't screwed on." There are many such opportunities to disguise your compulsions as more acceptable human foibles. Be vigilant in looking out for them.

Phil will snort. "If you want something to do with your hands, mate, you can have a crack at the dishes." Grace will silence him with a swift kick under the table and place her steady hand over the fluttering of your own. This moment of intimacy will be awkward for both of you but do not attempt to extricate yourself. Understand that she has inadvertently caught a wild thing and is now unsure as to the repercussions of releasing it.

When she rises, you will be in the home stretch. Helping her to clear the plates will be a no-brainer; any obsessive-compulsive worth his own salt can navigate the cracks between evenly spaced floor tiles through muscle memory alone. But now is not the time to let your guard down. Do not watch as Phil slips from his seat, removes the dishes from Grace's hands, and spins her in a clumsy circle before pressing her to him in a slow waltz. Do not listen as he croons Captain and Tennille's "Baby You Still Got It," his lips pressed to the space where her grey hair curls above her left ear. Concentrate instead on how Grace blushes and slaps his hand away from the small of her back. "Oh, you," she will say, smoothing her skirt and gathering the dishes for the second time (she is not smiling if you choose not to see it). Do not wonder how it would feel to lay down your numbers and rigid lines and step blindly into this world of bumps and soft curves, to not preface each action with a plan, each thought with a rule. Just follow her to the kitchen—placing one foot after the other—each landing squarely in the middle of every third tile.

"The Neurotic's Guide to Navigating Breakfast" originally appeared in *The Sleepers Almanac No. 9.*

The Polar Bear

by Jennifer Givhan

*I'm just another asshole sitting behind a desk writing about
this—*Facebook status update

What I'm asking is will watching The Discovery
Channel with my young black boy instead
of the news coverage of the riot funerals riot arrests
riot nothing changes riots be enough to keep him
from harm? We are on my bed crying for what we've done
to the polar bears, the male we've bonded with on-screen
whose search for seals on the melting ice has led him
to an island of walruses and he is desperate, it is late-
summer and he is starving and soon the freeze
will drive all life back into hiding, so he goes for it,
the dangerous hunt, the canine-sharp tusks
and armored hides for shields, the fused weapon
they create in mass, the whole island a system
for the elephant-large walruses who, in fear, huddle
together, who, in fear, fight back. This is not an analogy.

The polar bear is hungry, but the walruses fight back.
A mother pushes her pup into the icy water
and spears the hunter through the legs, the gut,
his blood clotting his fur as he curls into the ice
only feet away from the fray—where the walruses
have gathered again, sensing the threat has passed.
My boy's holding his stuffed animal, the white body
of the bear he loves, who will die tonight (who
has already died) and my boy asks me if this is real.
What I'm asking is how long will we stay walruses,
he and I, though I know this is not an analogy.

"The Polar Bear" originally appeared in *Rattle.*

Bartlesville, Oklahoma, 1980
by Barbara Dahlberg

The summer before you were born
was the hottest in 100 years.
With no place to go your father and I
moved into a tiny white farmhouse
with his sister Jean.

We overstayed our welcome
by at least two months.

The garden shriveled and burned
no matter how much I watered.
Under the straw mulch lay toads
splayed and bloated with water.
Locusts came and ate the few surviving plants,
even flew off with my dog Buddy's food,
nugget by nugget.

The wind blew red grit
onto every surface, into every bite we ate
sitting on webbed lawn chairs
in the living room
after Jean moved out,
took the tables
the couch
and the T.V.
Before she left her dog killed Buddy.

Alone in the evenings,
I sat on the porch swing
holding my belly
waiting for a breeze.
Birds nested on top
the rotten wooden pillars.
Beaks and bird bones
poked from holes
near the bottom.
Every night I watched
the taillights recede
as plumes of dust followed
your Dad to the bar.
I'd find him in the morning
face down in the dirt
somewhere between the porch steps
and the open truck door.

Letters home described
scissor-tailed flycatchers,

magical skies where stars
touched the ground,
the Milky Way a solid path.

"Bartlesville, Oklahoma, 1980" originally appeared in *Chapter and Verse*.

Triangle Shirtwaist Factory: March 25, 1911 Sestina

by Megan Gilmore

A bove us, between brick buildings, our ashes still fall
to sidewalks. Feathering down they catch in my mouth
like gray snow melting in our open palms, in our open
eyes, trying to clothe the end of all of us.
Beside me in the street another woman spreads
out, a snapped arm across her carbon face.

An hour ago we were sewing, the room all open—
an endless hall of cotton spreads.
A nearby woman wiped the sweat from her face
and then so did I, as our floor's collective dry mouth
licked its lips and returned to work–*don't fall
behind.* No one stopped to look at the street
or the sky, not one of us.

And then I smelled sulfur and smoky blue spreads
of linen. Shirtwaists on tables lit up for us
and danced a line of fire across the room to open

a flame on tables, chairs, and curtains—
which, heavy with heat, had to fall.
The fire leaped to walls, chewed the ceiling, its full mouth
licking up plaster with an angry face.

We shouted, pushing at the handle.
Hands ripped other hands to open
the door. Locked. One girl cried out—
we're on the tenth floor!—her face
so wide with terror I thought her mouth
might crumble and fall
between the floorboards. We crowded by the door—
help us! God help us!—
someone's bones cracked from our weighted spreads

of panic. Its sway so heavy that it threw us
against walls, onto the ground. I fell
to my knees and crawled around towering spreads
of fire that grabbed at my hair, my sleeves, face.
Then we saw the windows.
We ran and broke the glass, each mouth
sucking in relief as bloodied hands pushed into the open

sky. I heaved in air, my mouth
gasping as if after water.
We stood at windows, our collective face
numb with sweat and soot.
And then we jumped: arms outspread
like wings unexisting. Pedestrians below watched open-
eyed as we dropped like drunk, red leaves.
Unable to break our fall,

or rake us up. Now, too relieved to notice death,
I tumble away with the rest of us.

They are still coming down,
ashes that used to be a face, a mouth;
ashes that catch in wind and spread across town;
parts of me to fall on another street.
Open your door, Manhattan, and sweep us off your steps.

Vocabulary Lesson

by Don Hogle

My father is driving. I'm in the
passenger seat of the Rambler.

He watches the road. I look
straight ahead at the palm trees.

This is how we talk. How the
mysteries of sex were revealed

on Forest Hill Boulevard, how
the terms of my quitting Boy Scouts

were hashed out on Parker Avenue.
Today, as we head down Jog Road,

I say something is "exquisite."
His body angles away from me

as he makes a turn. I hear anger
in his voice when he says: *Boys*

don't use that word. We sit
in silence at the stop light on

Lake Worth Road, a hedge of red
hibiscus in full bloom beside us.

"Vocabulary Lesson" originally appeared in *Pooled Ink.*

Saratoga Passage, August 2014
by Matt Hohner

Whidbey Island, Puget Sound

Up late, I watch the Perseids etch their brief furies
through high, cold, moonlit air. My wife of eleven
years, partner of twenty-one, sleeps in the room behind me.
Three stories down, the salt tide slides away from concrete
bulwarks, slips quietly back into itself: the air's fragrance
leavens with life and decay as twelve hours of water give
way to rocks maned with kelp, sand rivulets emptying
under carcasses of hundred-year-old driftwood,
and the distinct whiff of an uneaten fish, speared
by talons and dropped, bottom-sunk until now.
In two days I will be forty-three. I know nothing
of my birth, hold no narrative of my making, nothing
of the weather that day, what you wore, who drove you
to the hospital. Above, particles ricochet in skips
and scratches through the dark emptiness between stars.
I must have been like these: a brief interrupter of cycles,

growing for nine moons, released out of you and away
into space, gone but for an umbilical scar, fading
into the sea of darkness and memory, covered by the
rhythm of tides, washed by time into something smooth
you carry, but cannot touch. A loon at the bend trills across
glassy currents; sound of wingtips in flight touching calm
water. The soft heartbeat of waves lapping the receding
tideline grows fainter as the frozen cosmos delivers hot
specks into fleet fire. I listen as ocean and moon sway
their eternal slow dance, one drawing the other closer,
then releasing. I have known this pulling-to and letting go,
the profound momentary ripples, the desolate stillness
that follows. I have known the searing white heat
of entry into this world alone.

Mascot

by Jeanne Julian

You got me through the audition.
    "Just keep moving," you said.
And so my wings flapped and flapped,
my feet hopped and hopped,
while the lone trombonist
from the pep band played
"Onward Mighty Fighting Owls"
woozily without
the snare for rhythm—
marking time was up to me.
But it all came together at VIC—TO—RY
when I pointed heavenward
with each syllable, like you told me to.
I think that clinched it.

And so I'm here for every game,
shape-shifter in this loose
acrylic custom costume,

more bear than bird,
but the floppy yellow talons
lend verisimilitude.
My brain keeps all its thoughts within
this outsized skull of durable
lightweight plastic. Gesture is all.
The only words permitted
past my sewn-shut beak
are the mascot chant: "Who, whoo!"

"Who" much concerns me these days.
You in the stands with who knows who.
Me down here frolicking with cheerleaders
who bounce, flail, and cry out
in their own skins and little else.
And who have I become,
dancing clumsily among them?
They hang in midair,
pentangles with bare midriffs,
kneel and mount each other
in a tempting pyramid
I long to topple as I bob around them.
Dear wife, I fear
The Official Owl Code
of "team loyalty and spirit, and
good fun" gradually is beginning
to outweigh the vows whoever I was
five years ago led me to make with you.
In rehearsal, Monique sensed the human
hand inside my plush appendage
as it brushed her thigh.

"Who do you think you are?"
she said, glaring up at two vinyl disks
inches above the holes through which
my real eyes peered. An offense
dreamed of, yes, but unintended,
incomplete,
fur muffling even my apology.

In constant motion on the field,
I realize you too must be tired,
clapping or (I'm too far away to tell)
merely surrounded by applause for me,
flapping my weary arms,
working the crowd, anonymous,
jolly, vigorous, and mocked,
in pantomime of flight, incapable
of taking off, sidelined between
the watchers and the watched.
Rooting for strangers
with a passion disproportionate,
I sometimes wonder
who'll cheer for you and me;
what Willendorf Venus or Penates
might shed stone for flesh and shout,
"Hang in there! 'The best is yet to be!'"
as after the game
we silently trudge to the car,
my head slung under my wing.

Art

by Eric Nelson

October, a woman and a boy, a tumor
Overtaking his brain, draw pictures
In the waiting room.

She makes a red apple as round
As a face. Then from her hand a cloud
Grows and darkens over the apple

Until the crayon breaks inside
Its wrapper and hangs like a snapped
Neck from her bloodless fingertips.

He's drawn two stick-figures
Up to their necks in falling gold
Leaves, their heads all smiles.

It's you and daddy, he tells her.
Above them a flock of m's
Fly toward a happy sun.

When she doesn't answer
He says on Halloween he'd like
To be a horse with orange wings.

Staring at his picture, she says
It looks like Thanksgiving.
Where are you?

He taps the sun, *I'm shining on you.*
She hugs him as if trying
To press him back inside her.

I'm not crying, she whispers.
He looks over her shoulder.
I'm not crying, too.

"Art" originally appeared in *Bellevue Literary Review*.

Choice of Words

by Valerie Nieman

My father and I
each became single
in the same year.

He is *bereft*,
robbed of his happiness,
a widower, or widowman.

His life has come undone,
and he is adrift
among the wreckage.

The only words worthy
of his loss are Anglo-Saxon
uncensored howls.

*

But I am *separated*
on the way to *divorce*,

terms for a civilized
coming apart.

Separated like an egg,
occasionally messy

but with some care
the yolk rests aloft,

while the white goes
cool and sliding into the bowl.

*

In plain words,
it's all butchery,

whatever the parting:
disjointed, sundered, severed.

*

A separation is also,
however, embarkation.

We stand at the rail,
each waving a white handkerchief
at the sinking shore.

Autumn, Six Months Later

by Michael Pearce

That night the whole city got quieter
as her puppy breathing quit forever
and her great hungry generous six-foot soul
relaxed into the starlight and sea noise
leaving faint images on walls and skin
leaving its last fingerprints on our tired backs.

When you watch your mother die
all you can do is die with her
and then there is no stopping, you are forever
dying toward someone you will never touch again
and there is no more waiting between thoughts
because the first and only life has ended in you.

When my mother died you rocked me in the bosom
of your voice rocked me in the voice of your good heart
and in the heart of our old love I slept,
alone and cared for, surrounded by her house
and the endless lament of the frogs out back
and a new sound, which is this world without her.

You send maple leaves from Massachusetts
to cheer me up saying the days since her dying
are like leaves fallen on her face,
and I bury you in a pile of words to push back the terror
of what's to come, to trap you at the very edge
of my life, remembering that

you stood outside my mother's cancer room
and shook with losing her
knowing the hearthstone of our family
has shattered, there is no one left to hold us
and the bed she died in
has closed its womb and heart.

I see you naked in the wet rot of fall leaves
see you nursing the snails and bugs with your dead blood
and I want to die with you
not now, but in the slow way that old lovers
learn the walk of humility and the breath of gratitude
together, as the mirrors sag into God's last word.

"Autumn, Six Months Later" originally appeared in *Ascent*.

Jealousy

by Mark Ramirez

The freedom of birds is an insult to me
—Cormac McCarthy

Cold drains from the sky
a minute at a time. Sunrise surfaces,
the only witness to a rusty pellet gun
half-cocked on the carpet.
Outside a dead sparrow has its wings spread
over the gravel surface of our driveway.
My dad sleeps in the living room chair,
beer-drunk, grabbing each breath
like last call before the lights
kick on. I shovel the bird
into a plastic bag, thinking about
why my dad had to take its life,
why he had to leave the morning
with one less song. Right before I leave
the front drive for school, I see him stir—

eyes half-shut against the light,
face still folded into the leather of bad sleep.
Later it's an hour drive to Detroit
where he will work into the night
installing windshields in the packed air
of an assembly plant. Twelve years
with the company, another twenty to go.
When I failed my entrance exam for Jeep
he told me he was glad. Can you blame him
for wanting wings?

"Jealousy" originally appeared in *San Pedro River Review*.

Faith in Love and Quantum Physics
by Brittney Scott

In one, my brother's in the gutter,
literally, face up almost floating along

second street after a hard rain, the clouds
finally clearing, the clean stars directing

traffic, his indelibly dirty palm planted
around a forty, which, in this life,

is all he ever drank.
In another, my brother isn't wrecked.

He owns a headshop on California's forgiving coast.
He has a beard, the tattoo of his nickname

retouched to add a vine of morning glories
for his wife, Glory, who watches home movies

of when he, *we*, were kids. What's important
is that he isn't dead in all of them. String Theory

suggests there are unlimited universes
exploding every second on top of each other,

each one different, a single action reversed,
rearranged, vastly, to slightly different.

He still dies in some, in many, but so do I.
He shoots me and then himself,

and we both disperse, keep running
in so many other directions that it doesn't matter

how bad it hurts. He's just an asshole
most of the time. I've even stopped talking to him,

cut off all communication after he stole my car,
stole my wedding ring for heroin,

whatever he's done. *I have no brother,*
I say to my friends at dinner parties.

Which is a privilege given
only to those who have them to disown.

I straighten my high-collared dress,
think of him out there, somewhere,

anywhere, but where this life keeps him now.
I stare out the window at my face half-hidden,

half reflected in the glass and the shifting ring of light
left on at the end of the walk.

Reparations
by Luke Wortley

Inside the fireplace there is a magnolia seed. Inside the magnolia seed there is a princess. Inside the princess there is a barbed-wire fence. Inside the barbed-wire fence there is Einstein's Theory of General Relativity. Inside Einstein's Theory of General Relativity there is a pitbull. Inside the pitbull there is a rope swing. Inside the rope swing there is a preacher's son. Inside the preacher's son there is an oil rig. Inside the oil rig there is the Mausoleum at Halicarnassus. Inside the Mausoleum at Halicarnassus there is a rhinoceros. Inside the rhinoceros there is a paisley purse. Inside the paisley purse there is Mammoth Cave. Inside Mammoth Cave there is God. Inside God there is a kudzu bloom. Inside the kudzu bloom there is an apology.

Newtown, Hearing

by Elaine Zimmerman

—for *Ally*

She heard the sounds from the school window.
A tapping from across the fields. Ten times.
What was that? A plane. A dream. So fast
she could only imagine river's thunder at
the unknown juncture, turning on itself.

A night train speeding past the window.
Some tired rider wishing for warm tea and bed.
Maybe a stallion leaping over the gray fence,
wildly charging. The muscle and rigor of
beast pushing past barn, elm, meadow.

Nothing like this could be the sound of
chaos running forward through bones,
a lost ring, one heap of marbles. They said it
was not possible to hear from so far away.
But of course she did. So did her friends.

Even the oaks bent forward to cape the
seeded soil. Orioles warned, on low-hanging
boughs, all tiny critters who dug into holes.
They already knew, of course. The light
had dimmed; the breeze changed.

Twenty children falling fast like stars.
Open armed and scattered. What would
have been play, if the spinning only
stopped or the season lurched right
into reason. But nothing gave meaning.

No. Winter's balance gone and splayed.
Ashen in the simple morning light.
She heard the sound from the school window.
A tapping from across the fields.

"Newtown, Hearing" originally appeared in *Theodate*.

Promises

by Hilary Dean

It was hard to explain.

"These roses are like … a … representation? Of like—"

"Hang on. No offence, Adrian, but it looks like you just got a bunch of flowers and put them all around your apartment and then they all died and you just took a picture of it."

"Yes. But actually, these roses—"

"It's trite. Is it trite on purpose? Is it a comment on banality?"

It was hard to explain my photograph during the critique because no one could shut their stupid fuckface mouths for even one second. The class was called *Theories of Representation* but it should have been called, *A Room Full of Assholes Think You are Dumb.*

There were a million assignments in art school and you were supposed to come up with meaningful art for all of them, even a photography theory compulsory you never wanted to take in the first place. They were *making* me take it. I wasn't even *in* Photography because I sucked at it, obviously. I was in Film. Totally different. But you had to take everything no matter what you specialized in. You think Fine Arts is going to be a bird degree and then you have to take classes all through the summer and talk about art until you want to kill yourself and also everyone else.

"It's cheesy. Dead roses. Dying love."

"It's not about love, you guys. It's about ... like ... Euhhh."

I stopped trying to explain and started not caring, which was much easier. They didn't mean to be mean. They just had to say smart things in front of the teacher to seem smart.

"Just so beyond clichéd."

Or they were all cockfaces, I don't know. I wasn't any better. I lied all the time in the opposite way because I wanted people to like me. I always said something positive even if I was ambivalent about someone's art installation or experimental film or shitty band. My ex-boyfriend Greg used to call me out on it all the time. *You're so fake,* he would say. He would do a dead-on high-pitched wide-eyed imitation of me. *Oh, I thought your film was great. So good. Those theatre students were really talented. I really believed they were dead. That blood looked really authentic. You make the best blood, what's your secret? Oh, cherry Kool-Aid, ohhhhh.*

Outside, it was bright and hot and ten million squirrels were running around like crazy. City squirrels are scary. They're all demented from a diet of Styrofoam and a life of narrowly escaping death. Each one is a mangled survivor of savage violence, with matted fur and scabby patches of skin. The ones downtown were always missing an eye or an ear, or a whole entire tail.

They scurried up the trees and across the shoulders of Egerton Finchaven, eponymous founder of the college, forever immortalized as a bronze pigeon-shit-covered squirrel sentry. His expression suggested a tranquil bliss, and from his right arm, earnestly extended in frozen mid-gesture, dangled a lacy pink bra. The bra had hung there for months, and was not a random act of vandalism, but an art installation homage to American college movies. Some jerk had gotten an A for it and I was jealous.

I could tell by the sun that it was just past three. I had a geography teacher in high school named Mr. Ludwig who was obsessed with the altitude of the sun. He made us learn to calculate it down to the decimal point with a protractor. He promised that it would come in handy if we got lost or stranded, as if we were foolhardy Sea Captains on weekends. But then I found myself breaking the sky into angles any time I was outside and the habit continued. I missed high school. I liked it when answers were just right or wrong and no one thought you were shallow because you took pictures of flowers and had all of Adam Sandler's movies.

On my way home, I stopped at the drug store to get makeup for my blandy pie face, bandages for my bloody knee gash, garbage bags for my gross apartment, and condoms because even though I was a mess, I was also still an optimist.

Outside my door, there was a bouquet of red roses. As I stared at them, my neighbor Elizabeth came down the hall with her terrier, who jumped all over me.

"Down, Ricki Lake! Hi, Adrian."

"Hi."

The dog had red nail polish on. I looked to see if Elizabeth had matching, but her nails were plain.

"You're so lucky," she said, looking at the roses. "Getting flowers all the time."

I smiled and shrugged like a cartoon, with jaunty shoulders and upturned palms.

"Yeah." *So fake, Adrian.*

Elizabeth sighed. "When I was twenty, I got flowers too."

I nodded the nod that you nod at the people that you see every day, instead of saying goodbye. I carried the flowers inside, dropped my purse on the floor, and opened the box of garbage bags.

I was twenty and I got flowers. My apartment was filled with red roses. There were ancient arrangements in yellowy water and shriveled variety store trios in plastic cones. Some were long-stemmed and solitary with sharp triangle thorns. There were a few velvet newborn babies like the ones just delivered but most had brown petals tinged with pink, beyond dead and crusted with decay.

I put the garbage bags in the cupboard. I wanted to throw the roses out but I couldn't just yet. They were innocent. They had nothing to do with any of it.

And where to start, even if I could? Most of the roses would seem, to an objective observer, inarguably gross and unfit for display. Others slightly less so. But where was the cut off? Medium-dead? Or at the first hint of imperfection? And who was I to say that some flowers were less perfect than others? Weren't they all interesting to look at in some way, if you laid aside your expectations of a better, lovelier flower? If you could forget, for just one second, your impossible ideals?

"Whore!" A man screamed from the sidewalk under my window. "Fucking whore!"

I hit the play button on my CD player and rolled the volume to max before remembering that it was empty and that all my CD's were destroyed. I turned on the TV and started rolling a joint.

"Slut! Where were you last night? You didn't sleep here last night, you whore!"

I'd gone a whole year without drugs of any kind, since Greg had been militantly anti-them. But after we'd broken up I'd started smoking weed again because it made being stalked by him more relaxing.

"Who was it, whore? Who were you with?"

I had been with Wes the night before. I was still feeling weird about it. I felt weird after it happened, and as it was happening, and definitely before he tied the condom in a knot, slingshotted it into the trash can across the room with a practiced arcing trajectory, kissed me and said, *Promise things won't be weird between us now?*

"Adrian!"

I got up and closed the window. People yelling my name was super embarrassing because of *Rocky*.

As I smoked, I wove an intricate mummy-lattice of bandages around my wasted knee. Then I grabbed five garbage bags from the cupboard and filled them with roses. It took a long time because I had to take several breaks in order to stare into space for no reason and by the time I finished it was getting quite late. I had to get ready for work that very second, or call in sick to the restaurant. If I called in sick I could avoid seeing Wes. But if I stayed home then I would be at home.

I brushed my teeth and washed my face. I hadn't cleaned since the fight, and the corpses of my murdered makeup were all over the bathroom. Delicate eyeliner pencils snapped in half, sweet lipstick stalagmites squished to pink mud. A shiny plastic uterus trailing the black ink of its mascara wand abortion. White porcelain stained with blue shadow. Glass fragments from a vial of concealer that splattered the walls the color of my skin when it smashed.

"I'm sorry," I said, as I dropped the pieces into the garbage. "I'm so sorry that this happened to you."

I opened the mirrored cabinet above the sink and reached for my pills. One for depression, two for anxiety. I swallowed them with a hand trench of water from the tap.

I couldn't call in sick because then they'd be shorthanded. Well guess what, I didn't care if they were shorthanded, fuck those assholes. But if I did call in sick, I'd spend the rest of the night imagining all the accidents that were happening that wouldn't have happened if they hadn't been shorthanded.

I could deal with seeing Wes. I could pretend that things weren't weird. I'm not the kind of actor who could emote on a stage with people staring at me, but I'm good at acting like a nice, normal person even though I'm actually a very terrible, shitty person.

I got dressed in my black shirt black skirt uniform and then put my new make-up on. I locked my door, took the stairs, and ran out of the lobby as fast as I could. When I looked back over my shoulder, I saw that Greg was running after me but I wasn't worried. I had a good lead.

Even after two months of following me everywhere, he hadn't built up the cardio to keep up with me. He had no physical endurance and wore tight corduroy pants. When we were together, I'd never judged him for being un-athletic, only for being delusional about it. He'd do this thing, like when he'd help me and the film kids carry equipment, or after draining a boiling spaghetti cauldron into my parents' kitchen sink. He'd pat his arms and say, *I have very powerful upper body strength. Built up from years of canoeing.*

People would nod with blank-faced politeness. All you had to do was look at him to know that he was lying. To officially confirm that the last time he'd ever canoed was at summer camp ten years ago, leaving more than a decade of Kazantzakis-reading stasis for any muscles he might have had to atrophy into the white speckled fish flab you saw be-fore your eyes.

I dodged people on the sidewalk with my patented ninja stealth. I sprinted across Wellesley Street and ran down the stairs into the subway. The doors of my train closed and I felt relief spill down my spine like a divine waterfall made from the tears of angels. Across from me, a man and a woman were making out with loud slurping mouth sounds. Out of courtesy, I changed seats so that I wouldn't murder them.

Walking toward the restaurant, I could see Wes and Ev the sous chef standing by the alley, smoking. I felt my asshole clench.

Wes was a sexy pasty white boy comedian. He treated me in two different and very specific ways. He was either sleepy-eyed hungover and annoyed by everything I said or hyper-attentive; laughing at my jokes, asking about my dreams, giving me head out of nowhere in the storage room at work. One mood was worth putting up with for the other mood.

He was amazing onstage. He had a sweetly mean candy punk confidence that drew people to him, made people want to please him. After each show, he'd have a dozen Toronto-coy suitresses pretending not to wait for him at the bar. His act was smart and twisted and I was attracted to the sweaty, earnest energy of it, which I had expected would translate into the heights of frenzied ecstasy during our ultimate coitus. Which was not what happened.

Here's what happened: Everything up until the act of penetration was great, you can go ahead and use your pervy imagination for that part, you giant perv. Then I was on top and I was just about to come. I was on the glorious precipice of coming. And then, without a hint of probing suggestion, without any warning or lubrication, he jammed his finger straight up my asshole. The sudden jolt of ripping pain took me right out of the moment, right out of everything. I made a terrible noise but his stupid face below me was oblivious. He came. I watched him come. This all happened in one single second in slow-motion and then it was over. I got off him and I was lying there staring at the ceiling like ... *Whaaaat just happened?* And I looked at his stained yellow scurvy pirate fingers with their jagged untamed hawk talons and I was furious.

Not even about the pain. The pain was only a sparking ember of hurt by that time. But the loss of my pleasure was an agony that burned through my body with the raging fire of a thousand hells.

He smiled. He kissed me. He was sweet to me. And all I could think was, *Get your finger out of my ass, Wes! Get your finger out of my ass, Wes!* But it was too late to say that. And then he said,

"Promise things won't be weird between us now?" And I was like,

"Yes." But I was lying. He said,

"Are you sure? Are you sure things won't be weird?" and I was like,

"Yes," but I was lying again.

You have to talk about these things, buddy. You have to communicate, I said to him, in my mind the day after.

"Hi," I said to Wes and Ev, in a normal way that was not weird at all.

"Adrian," said Ev, "Greg's here. He's at table nine."

"What?" I said. "He can't be here. He couldn't've gotten here so fast."

"He took a cab," said Ev. "We saw him pull up."

"He's a resourceful young man," said Wes. He offered me a cigarette from his pack and I took it. "You should go home, Aidge. We'll cover."

"Yeah," said Ev. "We'll tell them you looked sick."

"You looked terrible," said Wes. He smirked and reached out to light my cigarette for me, cupping the space around it with his hand. "But seriously, Adrian. Don't you think it's time you went to the police?"

*

"Where is he from?" laughed Yolanda. I was flopped on the couch in her mom's basement, melting my sweaty legs on its leather cushions and then peeling them off to feel the suction. She unwrapped the BLT sub I'd brought for her, took a bite, and spoke with her mouth full.

"Where is he from, this guy, where the police aren't dicks?"

"I don't know. Oshawa."

"The police, as if. Like they're going to care about Greg, that scrawny Amish-looking wankfest."

She poked a stray tendril of lettuce inside her sub with a gold fingernail.

"I knew the *first* time I met him, you know. We *all* knew. We all *hated* him."

"I know, Yolanda."

"You should have listened to me."

"I know."

"Because I *knew*." She clutched my arm. She had a habit of clutching arms. She touched people too often and too intensely.

"That night at the diner when he said he hated *Harold and Maude*?"

"Yeah."

"Who hates *Harold and Maude*?" Yolanda slammed her ginger ale down on the table.

"I know."

"What kind of horrible evil monster hates *Harold and Maude*?" She was screaming now, spitting sandwich blobs

91

everywhere. It was her second-favorite movie, after *The Year Punk Broke.*

*

I had an appointment with Dr. Nikhil. She had been my doctor for years and I loved her. I felt so at ease with her I'd thought nothing of going to her about my hymen situation three years before. I had met the handsome English teacher (not my school, it's allowed) who was going to deflower me and I wanted to know—was I stretched out already from tampons and ballet, or was I going to rip apart and bleed all over the place, Old Testament style?

When I'd gone to her for my panic attacks, I told her I was stressed out about school and sad about The Environment. She asked if there was anything else in my life that was a stress factor apart from school. *No.* She asked if I was doing any recreational drugs like marijuana. *No.* She asked if I was getting enough sleep. *No.* She asked if my parents knew what was going on with me. *Yes.*

Lie, lie, truth, lie.

"So, it's been six weeks now. How are you feeling?"

"I feel sad," I said. "And bad."

"Bad, how?"

"I feel pain," I said. "There's pain all over. But at the same time, I can't isolate it. I don't know where it's coming from."

"Like an ache?"

"Yes. But it's sharper than that. It's like a sharp ache. And there's also a bubbling to it. Like a bubbling aching sharpness."

"I don't understand."

"I know. I'm sorry. It's hard to explain. It feels like the pain is under my skin but over my organs. In my blood or fluids. Maybe my veins. It feels like my veins are melting but with a sharpness? Like how it would feel if your blood was powdered glass. Flowing and melting and stabbing."

I looked at her hopefully, expectantly. This was the part where she'd smile and say, *Oh yes, that sounds like melty-stabbyveinyitis. Let me write you a prescription.*

Instead she frowned and asked if I was drinking enough water. She said I probably wasn't getting enough exercise. And then I looked at Dr. Nikhil and the way she was looking at me, and I realized that I didn't really know her at all. She was familiar to me, but I didn't know her. And I didn't mean anything to her. Not really. She had requisitioned my tonsillectomy, vaccinated me, and even swabbed the cells of my cervix. But there existed between us a chasm far deeper than any vagina.

"So the medication isn't working," she said.

"It was working," I said. "And then I think it stopped working."

"Okay. I can definitely help you with that. You were probably on too low of a dosage. So we'll increase ... (she paused to write on her notepad) ... that."

"Okay."

"And Adrian, these medications have to be carefully monitored. So promise me that you'll come and see me right away if there are any changes in your appetite or sleeping patterns."

"I promise."

Outside the pharmacy, I clenched the prescription between my teeth while I rummaged through my purse for my insurance card.

"How many times have I told you not to do that?" said Greg, emerging from the shadows like a vampire except not sexy and I guess immune to daylight.

"Stop holding things in your mouth like a fucking dog. Have some respect for yourself."

His beard had grown longer. He was wearing a stupid white shirt with stupid suspenders and a stupid tie and a stupid hat.

"Leave me alone, psycho," I said. "You have to leave me alone. Unless you're here to give me money for all my stuff you wrecked."

"I told you, I was throwing out your trash. For your betterment. For your growth as a person. All I've been trying to do is to help you, Adrian. But you never listen. You don't change. I mean, you're in film school and you can't even sit through *The Seventh Seal* without falling asleep."

"You hate me," I said. "Listen to what you're saying, you *hate* me. You follow me around, you scream outside my window, you trash my apartment, you destroy my things. That equals you hate me. So leave me alone. Stop sending me flowers, stop everything."

He put his hand to his chest as if there was a heart inside it that hurt.

"Adrian, I love you. Don't you understand? I love you despite all your flaws, despite all your failings. Love is too powerful to just throw away. But you did. And you ruined my life."

"Yes, I'm aware. Can I please go now?"

"You promised me that we would be together forever. And you broke your promise. So I just want you to know that when I kill myself, you're going to be the one who finds my body. That's my promise to you."

"Awesome. You have a great day now."

*

It was difficult to pay attention.

"What makes your main character different from any other rambling, self-obsessed protagonist? Why should we care?"

It was difficult to pay attention in screenwriting class when I sat across from Owen Cosgrove and spent the whole time thinking wicked-perverted thoughts about him. Every week, I'd tell myself to choose a different seat so I wouldn't be distracted. But then, for some reason, I never did.

"Well, she's a sixty-year-old prostitute addicted to crystal meth."

"And?"

"She's blind."

"And?"

"She's the only witness to her twin sister's murder."

"Okay, but, like, *and*? What makes us *sympathize*?"

You needed to say things in class to get participation marks. And it was a small class, only twenty-five people, so it was totally noticeable if you didn't participate in the script critiques. Plus, our desks were arranged in a tight circle to encourage "civilized liberal discourse" as well as the objectification of Owen Cosgrove.

"Wait a second. This guy's supposed to be the city's ace private detective, and you want us to believe that he's completely incompetent? That he's *living* with the serial killer but missing all the clues that are right in front of his face?"

"It's called an Unreliable Narrator, in case you didn't know."

"Thanks, I got that. But when you reveal who's behind the monastery massacre in the first act, the detective loses all credibility. If I already know it was his mother, I can't take it seriously."

"I took your mother seriously last night."

"You wish!"

"Stacey. Claire. Please."

Professor Adelman hardly ever intervened. She was dignified and reserved, defending the honor of our mothers and adjusting her watch in such a subtle way, as if she were only feeling for a pulse and happened to notice the time.

I should have been criticizing someone, but it was difficult to pay attention. I kept having flashbacks of the cop drama we'd shot a few months before. Owen Cosgrove had played the disgruntled janitor, and I got to strap a fake bomb to his sweating, lightly muscled chest. Except that soundstage was actually freezing so my memory must have added in the sweat? Anyway, as I wrapped tape around Owen's torso, I was making jokes about being all aroused, except I wasn't joking. And now I have sex dreams where I make him come just before the bomb goes off and we both explode and die.

It was wrong. Do you know what he did every single weekend? He read to the blind. *Voluntarily.* I'm not even kidding. I might as well have been jerking off to Mother Theresa every night, I'm so depraved.

There was a knock at the door. A delivery guy came in and said, "Flowers for Adrian Green?"

"Aww," said everyone. I watched a bouquet pass around the circle of desks and land in front of me. Red roses.

Everyone was looking at me. Owen was looking at me.

These roses were different. There was a scent wafting off of them, something strange and sulphurous.

"Adrian," said Adelman. "If you can put those away, I'd like to discuss your script, *The Horrible Whore*. I have to say, I was quite disappointed. It seemed as though you didn't put any real effort or thought into it."

Oh, because I didn't.

"Would anyone else like to say anything?"

As the vultures descended to feast on the dripping bounty of my failure, I imagined Owen Cosgrove naked, reading to the blind. They wouldn't know.

After class, he stopped by my desk.

"Do you want to grab a coffee?" he said. "And just like, walk around?"

I nodded. He glanced at the roses in their waxy pink wrapping.

"From your ex again?"

I was still nodding from the nod before, reading Greg's card. I smiled dumbly at Owen and dropped the card inside my purse. I gave the flowers, awkwardly, to Adelman for her desk.

"I can't keep them," I said. "You know, symbolness."

She looked at the roses and looked at me.

"Do you mean *symbolism*, Adrian?"

"Oh. Isn't it called symbolness when it's a bad symbol that doesn't work?

"No, Adrian. That is not a word."

The coffee shop lady didn't like me. It's like she could tell I was an awful person filled with terrible thoughts. I closed my eyes and listened carefully to the inflection of her voice as she spoke to Owen. *Okay. Just her personality. Same way with everyone.*

As I walked with Owen, he'd stop every so often to pick up garbage from the sidewalk. He'd carry it until we reached a receptacle to drop it into. Oh my god, so hot. Other people's random garbage.

He said that he liked my script. He was lying to make me feel better because he thought I felt bad about the critique. But I didn't feel bad about the critique, I felt good because he was lying to make me feel better.

"Where do you want to go now?" he asked. "Is there anywhere we could find a bomb that you could strap on me?"

I laughed. And then I said a laugh. I said, "Ha ha."

Was he fucking with me? Because it was going to be very awkward going through life getting turned on every time I heard the word "bomb."

"You know where coffee tastes the best?" he said, "In my bed."

"Oh my goodness. You read to the blind with that mouth?"

*

There was too much pollen in the air. I needed eye drops every ten seconds for my allergies. But then I started seeing pollen dust indoors too, and that didn't make any sense.

"Yeah," said Yolanda. "I get that too. It's from all the acid we did in high school. Like optical flashbacks."

"Oh yeah, I've read about that."

We were crawling around her bedroom floor cleaning up grains of rice that had fallen out of our hair and our Rocky Horror outfits.

"Yolie, have you noticed all these people now who are wearing black jogging suits to Rocky? Why is that a thing now? Like, why can't they make an effort? Look at us, we look amazing."

I was Magenta, she was Dr. Scott.

"Fuck," she said, "I wish we had some acid right now."

"Me too, fuck."

There was no acid anymore. The hippies were all gone, and kids in the news were dying from taking fake acid poison.

I slept with Sebastian from photography class. He had beautiful bug eyes and exquisite squid lips.

He said, "I really like you. But you're not my type. No offense."

"What's your type?"

"I like farm girls. I like heavy boots and lots of plaid. And of course she would have to be vegan."

"That's impossible," I said. "Vegans are so weak, they're like origami people."

He grunted, rose to kneeling, picked me up in his gorilla arms, and tossed me back down on the bed.

"Hey, your calendar's wrong, fool," I said, looking up at the wall. "It's not August yet."

"It's been August for weeks, Helen Keller."

"No. And your ex-girlfriend wasn't a farm girl. And she was only vegetarian."

"Well, she wasn't the one. When I find the one, she's going to be taller than me, older than me, and smarter than me."

"I'm smarter than you."

"No," he said, putting his smiling Bengal tiger face right up to mine. "You're like the biggest idiot."

Next day, I had a headache because of the squirrels. There were more squirrels than I'd ever seen on campus before, and louder than ever. Their twittering was frantic and unsettling; a mad chorus of sinister rodent songs about chewing people's faces off.

I was also super annoyed at all the tourists downtown. Smiling so happily. Staring at everything. Finding Toronto fascinating for some reason. And what strange foreign land had they travelled from where everyone wore black jogging suits but did not jog?

"Did Puff Daddy tell everyone that jogging suits were cool now?" I asked Owen.

"He's P. Diddy now," he said. "Try to keep up."

Owen snapped at me sometimes. He'd get mad for no reason.

At Yolanda's party, there were too many people hogging all the air inside her house. I hung out with Wes's friend Dylan on the front porch. He had dark hair and blue-grey eyes and his voice gave me sparkly brain shivers. Out of genuine concern, he asked about the scab above my knee (bike, dog, gravel) and gently moved aside the hem of my dress to inspect it. His innocent smile conveyed the caring sympathy of a friend, and when his hand grazed my leg, my vagina began frothing like it was rabid.

*

"Watch yourself," said Wes.

"Huh?" I was peeling potatoes. I didn't look up.

"Dylan really likes you. And he's my friend. You can't be stupid with him, Adrian. You can't be careless."

"He isn't a precious baby duckling, Wes."

"No, listen. He's a good person. He's too good for you."

"What does *that* mean?"

"It means you *suck*."

As I rinsed the potatoes, he sang the song *Daytripper* very casually, as if he were just singing it. It was a passive-aggressive way of calling me a skank, but it was a cute way of being passive-aggressive. Such a great song.

But then later, in front of the dishwashers, he casually asked me if vegan sperm tasted better than meat eaters' sperm. As if I was some kind of cum-gargling sewer-slut.

"Come on, Wes," I said.

"What? It's a scientific inquiry."

I knew that he knew what he was doing. That he was demoting me out of the category of women he would respect too much to publicly ask that question of, while disguising it as an expectation that I would be cool enough to answer it casually in these modern times. But by answering, I was volunteering myself for the category he would subsequently use as his excuse to not like me anymore—uptight bitch or stupid slut. And that was sad. He couldn't be nice because I was being weird after I promised that I wouldn't be—because of the lingering ass-finger ghost. But he thought that I didn't like him anymore, so he had to act like he didn't like me anymore. And that made me actually not like him even though I still kind of did. But when he looked at me all blank as if he'd never touched me anywhere at all, oh my god, I hated him so much.

"What?" he said. "It's just a question."

"Fine. Go fuck yourself."

He looked at me like I was crazy.

"Well, fuck you then. Uptight bitch."

My apartment was freezing. My landlady came up to check the thermostat and said there was nothing wrong with it. It seemed fine to her. I stood there wearing four sweaters and shivering, making small talk so that she'd stay long enough to feel the chill and start believing me. It was the blazing end of August and it felt like Planet Hoth.

Even worse, my neighbor across the street was spying on me, watching the whole thing. He was probably the one messing with my heat too, as some kind of entertainment for his own amusement. What a petty, cruel thing to do to a person. To use them as your own little science experiment as if their life was nothing. Fucking asshole. I couldn't sleep for six nights in a row because of him.

*

"Adrian," said Wes. "Eat this."

It looked like a plate of spaghetti but it smelled like rust.

"Why?" I said. "Who told you to give this to me? Where did you get it?"

"It's from the kitchen," he said. "Ev made it."

I looked over at Ev and she waved.

"Why?"

"Because you haven't eaten all day and you need to eat. You look sick and you're acting weird."

"No, I'm not."

I was not acting weird. I was acting very normal. I was acting very normal on purpose because this thing was happening where my thoughts were appearing in my head as words on paper. And as soon as I thought anything, the paper would start crinkle-burning at the edges. Then I'd have to start thinking new thoughts really fast to get another page before the last one burned. Considering that this was happening, I was doing an excellent job of holding it together. Considering this was happening and I had even come into work, I should have been given a congressional medal of honor.

It was Wes who was weird. I had evidence that would hold up in court. Exhibit A: The morning after we'd slept together, I was getting ready to leave but I had to step around a bunch of loose notebook pages that were scattered all over the floor.

"You have new material?" I asked.

"No." He was sitting at his desk wearing only blue boxers, editing a video on his computer with a lit cigarette in his hand. "That's just a letter some girl wrote me."

"Really?" I said, "There's like twenty pages here. What does it say?"

"I don't know," he shrugged. "I haven't read it."

"Don't you want to?"

He laughed. "No."

"Did she write on both sides? Did she number the pages? If I organize it and staple it together, will you read it then?"

He took a drag. "I'm pretty busy, Adrian." He blew the smoke out the side of his mouth in a thin stream. "I can't read every letter that every crazy girl writes to me."

I pushed the plate of spaghetti away. I looked up at him.

"You're so cool," I said. "How are you so cool?"

"Aidge, listen. If you're feeling sick, Ev said she can make you soup. Or even something from the weekend menu."

"I'm not cool at all. I'm not even cool one *bit*."

"Buddy, just eat something."

He handed me the menu. I blinked over and over, hoping that my eyes would focus. But it wasn't my eyes. The menu made no sense.

How was my neighbor doing this? He'd found out where I worked. He had access to expensive technology. No, there had to be a group of them to organize all this. A crew to install cameras. They were watching me read the menu to see how I'd react. I had to act normal, so they wouldn't know that I'd figured things out.

"I have to go," I said brightly. "I have to quit. Not because of you."

I took my apron off and grabbed my purse from the shelf.

"Because of something else," I explained.

Outside, I looked up and saw a body plummeting to the ground like a falling star. Before I could scream, my eyes pulled focus and there was nothing there. Only a shadow, or a bird, or a shadow of a bird or a bird of a shadow.

I found Greg's card in my purse, the one that came with the flowers. I read it again: *"I will always love you, Adrian. From the cradle to the grave."*

That doesn't even make sense, asshole. I didn't even know you when you were born and if I did I would have been a baby too, and babies don't know what love is, or at least they don't know a word for it from a language. And that's not even original, that's the *U2* song from *Reality Bites.*

I ripped the card into wretched snowflakes. I triangled my fingers and delicately seasoned the inside of my purse with them. Then I walked around the city. I walked and walked forever. I took all the tiny pieces of the card and dropped them into different receptacles on random streets. I got rid of them all. I lost track of time. I looked up to find the sun but there was no sun. Only grey.

It occurred to me for a moment that what I was doing wasn't normal behavior. It was superstitious and strange and not something that a strong, confident woman would do.

I once met a strong, confident woman on a train as we pulled out of the station in Savannah, Georgia. The English teacher I'd fallen in love with had moved there and I'd gone to visit him. When I left to go home, I was waving goodbye to him from the window and I was crying as the train pulled away and it was the most romantic moment of my life.

The woman beside me was wearing a Sea World souvenir baseball cap with a dolphin on it. She said, *Honey, is that your man? Just wave goodbye, honey, it's easy. I've said goodbye to lots of men. Just left them in the dust. And another one always comes along before the dust can even settle.* She made me laugh. She made the rest of the train ride so much fun, and she showed me pictures of Sea World, and I never forgot her. You think that Americans can't really be like how they are in movies, but they totally are.

Wait. What if instead of destroying the power of the card by separating its parts, I had increased its power exponentially by spreading the surface area it covered?

I reached for my pills. The bottle was empty. I had repeats though. Repeats repeats repeats.

"Drink lots of water," said the pharmacist. "And no alcohol while you're on this medication."

Yeah right, buddy. Yeah right yeah right yeah right.

Outside the pharmacy, there were more annoying people hanging out, wearing black jogging suits and watching me, smiling. They probably weren't tourists. They looked more like a boring theatre troupe or a sporty touring orchestra. And they knew my face now, from hanging out in my neighborhood all summer. They'd nod and smile at me but it wasn't pleasant, it was irritating. *Do you have a staring problem?* I wanted to say. *Stare much?*

*

Hot bug-eyed Sebastian took me to High Park for a picnic, which was really nice, really really really nice, I know, I know. But I couldn't eat any of his food. He said he wanted to prove to me that vegan food could taste like real, and I would love it.

"Just try it," he said, offering me a plate of white cubes. "Adrian, come on. Not even fruit? Not even a plum?"

"I'm not hungry."

What did he care if I ate or not? Why was it so important to him?

"Sebastian, did someone give you this food to give to me?"

"What do you mean? I bought it at the store."

"I'm just not hungry."

He had a Frisbee. He wanted to play Frisbee. He had this idea that I was the kind of girl who would run around on the grass and throw a Frisbee in the sun. He had his camera out because he wanted to take pictures of me doing this, pictures of having fun. But I was wearing heels and I had no energy and I just wanted to sit and smoke cigarettes with my back against a tree. He had this idea that I was a certain kind of girl and we'd have a certain kind of day. But it was so beyond never happening that I couldn't even try to fake it.

I had already ruined everything but I agreed to walk to the petting zoo. There were four majestic bison in a small pen. They had crusty fur and they smelled bad. They looked at me and they begged me to save them but I couldn't, I couldn't. And I felt so terribly sad because this was the worst, most devastating place on Earth, but the crowd of people all around us were smiling and laughing as if it were a nice place, a happy place.

"What do you think of this?" I asked Sebastian.

They had messed up and I'd caught them. A passionate vegan wouldn't like to go to a petting zoo. In fact, the whole afternoon had been full of urgent artifice, a poorly staged production of human romantic clichés. It all made sense. From the beginning, a part of me had always known that

Sebastian was too good-looking for me, too obviously out of my league. My question was the final test.

"What do you think?"

"I think it's nice," he said, "to say hi-son to the bison."

What the fuck?

*

They couldn't tamper with the headache pills because each bottle came with a silver seal and cotton stuffing inside that proved it hadn't been tampered with.

But they would know that I would be tricked by the illusion of safety, and they knew that what they were doing to me was causing headaches. And they would also know what drug store I usually went to, so I had to go to a different store.

But they would *expect* me to go to a different store. They were watching me and laughing at how predictable I was. They would have put their poison chemicals in the bottles at the new store, positioned in accordance with my height and my eye line. But would they know that I would anticipate this as well? Would they predict, based on the study so far, that I would always think I was a step ahead of them and therefore choose a bottle on a lower shelf? Would they have anticipated that I would thwart their strategic positioning, and then attempt to thwart my thwarting?

I heard an angry voice from the aisle behind me. I slowly walked around the corner to see who was talking. A man and a woman in the dental care section.

"*No*," said the man. "How many times do I have to *tell* you? The toothpaste with the *baking* soda, the dental floss with the *mint*, and the mouthwash with the long-lasting *flavor*."

"But I don't like the taste of baking soda," said the woman. "I like a sweeter toothpaste."

"Lorraine," said the man, "Do you want me to kiss you or not?"

"Run away, Lorraine!" I yelled.

Then I turned and ran from them, my head filled with boiling lava. A bearded man in a black jogging suit smiled at me obnoxiously as I ran past him and out the door.

*

It was painful to breathe. In the studio at school, I dragged paint across a canvas but it was difficult to paint. How had I painted before? I couldn't remember. Was I painting too slowly? Did this look like normal painting? Were Gerry and Claire whispering about how I was painting weird?

"Who's that?" asked Stacey. She leaned over to look at my canvas.

"Oh," I said. "This is my high school geography teacher."

I was painting Mr. Ludwig. Trying to get him right. Trying to re-create the blanked out peaceful expression he had, even when I was so rude to him. I had told him that solar geometry was useless in real life. I had promised him that as long as I lived, I would never need to calculate the altitude of the sun. I was obnoxious and bratty. He asked me to leave his class. He gave me detention. And then—

"They're going to kill you in Crit for this one. But I like it."

"Thanks, Stace. He wouldn't give me peace."

"What?"

"Mr. Ludwig. At school. We had a chapel in our school. And during mass—this is Catholic mass—there's a part where the priest tells everyone to offer each other the sign of peace. And it's a handshake. You shake people's hands who are sitting around you and you both say, *Peace be with you.* So I was doing that. And I turned around. And Mr. Ludwig was standing there, and I offered my hand to him. But he wouldn't shake it. He just stood there and shook his head, *No.* He wouldn't give me peace in church. In front of God and everyone. Because of how awful I was."

"Wow," said Stacey, "You've lost like a ton of weight, Adrian. You look awesome."

"Thanks."

A woman poked her head in the doorway and glanced around the studio as if she were looking for someone. She had grey hair and was wearing a trendy black jogging suit. She smiled at me, then walked out. Lost.

"Guys," I said. "Do you know whose dumb music video is shooting around here? All the people wearing black jogging suits and running shoes?"

"No," said Claire.

Stacey and Gerry shook their heads.

"There's all these extras hanging around the city and they're dressed in black jogging suits and sneakers and I hate them."

"You're talking so fast," laughed Claire. "Too much coffee, eh?

"It sounds like a performance art piece," said Gerry. "Probably the new media school is doing it."

"Oh," I said. I went back to painting. "New media is bullshit."

Ev invited me to see Wes's show. When I got there, I saw her sitting near the front of the stage but I stayed in the dark at the back by myself. He wasn't funny. I didn't laugh once. Other people were laughing but it was all fake. They were acting, acting like laughing people.

After his set, Wes headed toward the end of the bar where I was standing. Lots of girls smiled at him and waved to him, and as he walked through the room, he greeted each of them with a fond pat on the head.

When he got to me, I looked right at him and focused what I was thinking into my eyeballs which was, *If you pat me on the head, motherfucker, I will kick you in the balls.* But he turned his back and ignored me completely.

"Wes!"

He turned around.

"Get your finger out of my ass!" I yelled.

Then, obviously, I left.

The next morning, Yolanda and I were sitting on the smoking patio of the coffee shop when I looked across the street and saw a man in a black jogging suit staring at us.

"I'm so sick of these people," I said. "Like, find something to do. Okay, you know me, *hi.*"

I waved sarcastically. The man waved back with wide open eyes.

"What is that guy's problem?" I said. "Why is he being so creepy? Should we go somewhere else?"

"What guy? Who are you waving to?"

"That guy."

"I don't see anyone."

*

When I first realized I was going crazy, I did what I thought was a very sane thing to do. I went to the library for information, like I would have done normally if I was researching something normal. I figured, other people have gone crazy, so there must be lots of books on it and what to do about it and how not to be crazy anymore.

I knew exactly what I was looking for. The book would have a sky-blue cover with text in white italic cursive that said, *So You're Going Crazy...* and on the back would be a photograph of the author; a renowned doctor, an elderly man with soft white hair and a kind smile. He would look sort of like Kurt Vonnegut, and he would tell me not to worry, that everything was going to be fine, and here's what to do to control your brain and stop it from seeing these terrible things that no one else is seeing.

But my book wasn't there. And the self-help section was just rows of meditation and rainbows, and people on the covers holding out crystals like they could save you. I scanned the shelves with my head twisted sideways to read each individual spine. I flipped through books and spoiled their endings. Buddha, Krishna, Jesus, AA, naturopathy, hiking a very long trail for a very long time. No thanks, buddy.

There was one of them in the library watching me. Amused by me. He was real. I looked at him and I saw every wrinkle on his face and every crease in his jogging suit and he was real. There was no book that could help me.

There was only fear. And a sudden cold, sharp clarity. The universe was pulsing with dark secret things that I hadn't been able to see before. Now I saw everything. It was all perfectly clear.

There had been a mistake. I was supposed to have died already. They had been sent to collect me, to make things right. They would join me on the subway platform and point to the black pit of tunnel as a speeding train approached the station. On the street, they'd look up and point to bridges and fire escapes for me to jump off. They spoke very little. They spoke without speaking. They looked at me and filled my head with their words. *It's time, Adrian. It's alright. It's easy.*

They left messages for me. A dead bird on the sidewalk in front of my apartment, its insides oozing out red and pink. My initials spelled out in gothic clouds. The lit up yellow windows of a distant apartment complex forming a perfect X.

It's time.

I didn't want to die. But my head was filled with kaleidoscopic images of my death, simultaneous variations of scenes playing over and over until each one seemed both an inevitable future and an event in the past, as if I'd already died a thousand times and was only lingering inside a breathing bag of skin.

I wasn't sure how to do it. I was too scared to fall or drown or bleed. I had no way of getting a gun. Plus, there was the problem of leaving my body for someone else to find. I didn't want anyone to happen upon it and be traumatized forever. There had to be a creative solution, like exploding or disintegrating. The voices were big advocates of jumping. Of falling.

I didn't know what to do. There was nothing to do. Except lie on the floor of my apartment with my hands pressed to my heart and stay there for days and days and days.

*

There was a knock at the door.

"Adrian? It's Elizabeth."

Elizabeth. Okay. Okay. Okay.

I opened the door.

"Hi, Adrian. Hi. So, I was wondering? If maybe you could stop playing that song. That song you keep playing over and over? I'm sorry, I know it's probably for a school project or something. And I love David Bowie, of course. But any song, even the best song, when you hear it a thousand times…"

"Oh. Okay, Elizabeth. I'll turn it off. That's easy. That is not even a problem at all."

"Thanks, Adrian. You have a good night."

Dylan had lent me a pile of CD's but the one Bowie song was all I played. It wasn't homework for school because I had dropped out of school. The song was for not killing myself. It was for staying safe and not killing myself because my body had turned against me. My body had violent urges to go outside and step in front of speeding cars. It was pulling itself in terrible directions and the mind had to use all of its strength to stop it. It was difficult to control the body and drag it away from the dangerous magnets. It took everything I had and I was steadily weakening.

Inside my apartment, the body wanted to reach for knives and stab itself with them and swallow all the pills, so the mind threw away all the knives and the pills. Most of the mind was responsible and was trying to save everything. But part of the mind also wanted to die, just not as badly as

114

the body did. The body was relentlessly begging to die, although it had used its own arms to throw the dangerous objects away. I didn't know what was which part. Who was fighting to die and who was fighting to live? And which one was me? And who was going to win?

The song I kept playing was *Jump (They Say)*. But really, it's a song about not jumping. The words are about not killing yourself, but it was the melody of the synth hook that was saving me. It was the exact sound of the lure of falling, of giving in to the universe, of giving yourself to the sky. But by listening to that sound, you could hold that feeling inside you. You could swallow it down and hold it in your lungs and lock it in your heart and you could have it. You could neutralize the dangerous magnets, and watch all the scary things swirl around you while you stayed perfectly still.

I didn't have headphones. I needed a place where I could blast the song as loud as I wanted to, a place like my old bedroom at home that was now my mom's second office.

I called my mom. I told her that I was sick and I was taking a break from school and I wanted to come stay with her for a while.

"You sound strange, Adrian. Wait, are you doing a bit? Are you doing *Rain Man*? I love that movie."

I had this idea that home was safe. That they wouldn't follow me there. They would leave me alone because home was solid and clean and pure and good.

I took the bus up to Richmond Hill. Beside me, there was a man wearing headphones. He was learning English from a tape.

"Your mother is a lovely woman," he said. "Your mother is a lovely woman."

They knew where I was going. But they hadn't sent anyone on the bus with me and that was promising. Hopefully I was right and there was a force field at the border of the town that they wouldn't be able to penetrate. Probably at the welcome sign that said, *Home of Elvis Stojko*.

I stared out the window and watched the town materialize block by block.

"Your mother is a lovely woman. This photograph does not do her justice."

Forty-five minutes north of Toronto, the squirrels are fluffy and bouncy. At dusk, I'm not even kidding, wild bunnies hop across the lawns. Nothing bad can happen in front of bunnies.

My mom had ordered a whole table of Chinese food but I couldn't even eat one fortune cookie.

"What's wrong, Adrian?"

"Nothing. I'm fine."

"Then promise me you'll stay home tonight and rest."

"I promise," I lied.

It had to be that night. Home didn't mean anything. Geography didn't matter. They would never leave me alone.

My fortune cookie had been the final sign. Inside it was a white paper rectangle, blank on both sides. No fortune. No future.

I had a plan. I followed my plan. I waited until everyone was asleep, and then I silently left the house using my patented ninja stealth. I walked to the hospital. The same hospital where I had been born. Symbolness.

I went to the Emergency Room but I didn't admit my-self. I just sat there. The plan was to swallow all the pills I had left, all the anti-depressants and sleeping pills that had never worked.

From here, I could go directly to the morgue without bothering too many people. It would be just another death, a matter of routine for trained medical professionals.

I swallowed the pills. I drank from my water bottle. Then it occurred to me to leave a note. I found a pencil in my purse and a stray hospital leaflet that was asking for do-nations.

I didn't know what to write. I hadn't thought about it.

When someone commits suicide in a movie, they have a reason. They write the reason down in their suicide note. But I didn't have a reason. I just had to die, it wasn't even up to me. I knew, in a cloudy way, that people who loved me would have feelings of sadness about me being gone. But that was a minor inconvenience, a trivial detail com-pared to my pain. If they could have felt my pain, they would have understood.

But I couldn't write that. Because it wasn't even pain. That word was too small. My DNA had sharpened into stabbing microscopic helices, corkscrews piercing through my cells.

This feeling of needing to die was stronger than any feeling I'd ever felt. Certainly it was far more vast than any sadness. It was stronger than my love or my empathy for anyone. It blacked out all other emotions with such urgency that any trace of them within me was a mote of sunlight compared to a thousand haunted planets. It was a burning compulsion that eclipsed all else, obliterated all reason.

There was no such thing as a reason, anyway. Just as there was no such thing as a promise. A promise was only a word for a symbol of a concept in a dimension of a reality that didn't even exist.

But I couldn't write that either.

Peace out forever, I wrote.

*

I was sitting at a desk, alone in a room full of empty desks.

The door opened and an elderly man walked toward me.

"Where am I?" I asked him.

"You're in Richmond Hill, Ontario."

"Oh good." I said. "That's where I wanted to be."

The man was wearing a brown blazer with light brown patches at the elbows. He sat down in the chair opposite me.

"What day is it?" I asked him. "What time is it? I feel like I had an appointment or something. I'm supposed to be somewhere else."

"It's September 22nd."

"Oh," I said. "Mr. Ludwig. I didn't recognize you."

"Hello, Adrian."

"Hi. Oh. There's a test today and I didn't study. That's why I have this panic feeling. I'm supposed to take a test and I'm not prepared. I have dreams like this sometimes."

"It's alright. There's only one question. All you need to do is tell me the altitude of the sun."

I looked down at my empty hands.

"I can't, Sir. I can't see the sun. And I don't have a protractor or an atlas."

"You can do this. I promise. I'll help you."

"You will? Can you tell me the latitude of Richmond Hill?"

"Yes. It's 43.8729 degrees north."

On the desk in front of me there was a pencil and a leaflet. I wrote the number down. "And what time is it, please?"

"It is exactly noon. On the autumnal equinox."

"Okay. I know this one. That means the sun's rays form ninety degrees with the Earth."

"Yes."

"And the sub solar point is the equator. So, that's zero degrees. The altitude is the angle between the Earth and the sun."

"Good."

"Alright. Then, for every degree of latitude away from the sub solar point, the altitude decreases by one degree. Right? So I just have to subtract. That's easy. I can just do subtraction on this paper."

I printed as neatly as I could. I passed the leaflet across the desk to Mr. Ludwig. He held the paper up to the light and read it. He folded it and placed it in the pocket of his blazer. Then he held out his hand and I shook it.

"Peace be with you," he said.

Allomother

by Melanie Cheng

Sunday nights are for planning. I search the internet for the latest exhibits, concerts and other kid-friendly events. We've been to the core attractions: the museum, the botanical gardens, the children's farm, the gallery. We've sampled babycinos and avocado smash at all but the most pretentious cafes.

Sometimes I don't plan anything at all. I plan not to plan—because too much structure can suffocate creativity in a child—and we do silly things like make nappies for Dolly from the fallen leaves in my backyard.

Monday nights are for cooking. I bake homemade treats for our outings. Healthy snacks like apricot muesli bars and savoury muffins made with organic pumpkin and goat's cheese. There has to be something to counteract the frozen rubbish that gets dished up at home. *Snap frozen*, her mother corrects me, but she is just defending the time she spends on the couch, watching back-to-back episodes of *House of Cards*.

Tuesday nights are for packing. Or rather checking that my oversized, waterproof handbag is adequately stocked. Because, when it comes to kids—and Molly in particular— you can never be too prepared. Every so often I get caught out and have to add another item to my list. It's an organic thing, my list, a little like my muesli bars. *Two packets of Wiggles bandaids, one tube of Cancer Council approved nano-free kids sunscreen, a hat, a cardigan, a spare pair of underwear, a BPA-free water bottle, a Tupperware box with aforementioned organic snacks, face towels, Molly's second favourite Barbie doll (Candy, with the blue biro-coloured hair) and my camera.*

*

I have one photo. Jules and Mick took everything else— the ultrasound images and DVDs, even the positive pregnancy test I dipped in my urine. It's a selfie taken in the bathroom mirror, with one hand cupping my belly. The phone covers my face. Only my mouth is showing. I am wearing a grey maternity top from Kmart and a pair of black tracksuit pants covered in lint.

There are no identifying features. No scars or beauty spots or tattoos of ex-lovers' names. Nothing to prove that it is me. It could be anyone.

*

"I want to see the ephelants."

We are in the monkey enclosure. A female is nursing her newborn; two young chimps are catapulting from tree to tree; and a large male is lying on the platform-cum-stage, juggling his salmon-pink testicles.

Molly sucks her thumb. She is an elephant person, like her mother. Jules brought me a sandalwood one once, as a last minute gift, at Koh Samui Airport. But that was a long time ago. Back when she and Mick had money to travel. Before IVF, and the miscarriages. Before varicose veins, and Molly.

"Dara's waiting for me."

Dara is the new elephant calf. One of three conceived at the zoo.

"His name means star," Molly says, as we turn our back on the monkeys. "Like me!"

"That's right," I say, genuinely impressed. "Yours means star of the sea."

I don't mention the Hebrew meaning—and the reason Jules and Mick chose it in the end. *Molly. Diminutive of Mary: the wished-for one.*

*

They took vial after vial of blood. I was terrified but I needn't have been. My hormone levels were *within normal limits* and my uterus wasn't *hostile*—who knew organs could be hostile?—like my sister's. It was the proof I had been searching for all these years that I was better than her. But the victory didn't give me the joy I thought it would. I didn't feel like I'd won anything.

*

At strategic points around the zoo there are candy coloured signs spouting facts about the animals:

Did you know that elephant society has a female-led structure that is often called matriarchal? The oldest female is the matriarch. She determines the group's movements.

I try to explain the words to Molly—to convey the complexity of these awesome beasts—but she just hops on one foot and screams that she needs to wee.

*

It wasn't until I was being wheeled into theatre that any of us believed I might actually die.

"You'll be fine." The anaesthetist said but I didn't trust him. He was too good-looking to be a doctor.

I watched the painful shrink of Mick and Jules' faces as they pulled me along the corridor. They didn't wave—that would have been too much like farewell—they just stood very still. Only then did I see myself as they did: a vessel for their magic bean. For the first time, clutching each other as if they might drown in the linoleum sea, they looked the part: a mummy and a daddy.

*

I am drinking a watery cappuccino at the zoo cafeteria. Molly is under my chair, feeding discarded chips to a one-legged pigeon. It is three o'clock and the café is full. I scan the tables, priding myself on being able to pick the parents from the non-parents. The parents are the ones checking email on their smartphones while their toddler eats marshmallows off the floor. It's the Nannas and Pops and Aunties and Uncles who hang, bright-eyed, on every mis-pronounced word, confident they will soon be rewarded with a flash of wisdom or comedic genius. Like when Molly compares the mole on my neck to a sultana, or asks me questions I can't answer, like whether fish sleep and if they do how do I know if they never close their eyes?

*

Did you know that the main function of the family unit is the protection of baby elephants? The greater the number of females looking after a calf, the greater its chance of survival.

123

*

I looked at Jules and Mick across the expanse of polished mahogany.

"Just a formality hun."

The lawyer was an ageless Chinese woman who could pass for forty or fourteen. She nudged the thirty-page document towards me.

At birth, the Surrogate will relinquish the Child(ren) to the Biological Father and Biological Mother, and the Biological Father and Biological Mother will assume all parental rights and responsibilities for the Child(ren) from that time forward.

Twenty weeks. She was the length of a banana. Her ears were perfectly formed. I had just started to feel her dart like a slippery fish inside me.

"We wanted to wait." Jules said, as if reading my mind.

"To make sure it was viable." Mick explained.

"It?" I snapped and Mick went white. We had found out the sex at the last scan.

"*She.*"

Jules shook her head. The lawyer pulled a pen from her breast pocket. One of those old-fashioned fountain pens with a reservoir and a nib. She placed it in a ceremonious diagonal across the paper.

"I'm not going to steal your child."

"Of course not." Jules said but the baby-faced lawyer disagreed.

"Kids do strange things to people."

I looked at my sister's stony face and her husband's blotchy, patchwork one. I felt a flutter—the flap of tiny arms perhaps—in the fleshy space below my bellybutton. I picked up the pen.

"They sure do."

*

Dad took me and Jules to the zoo once. I must have been about thirteen. It was a big deal, coming down on the train from Bendigo for the day. We were celebrating Jules getting picked for the under 15s hockey team. Mum had to work but Dad, being a teacher, was off for the school holidays.

I don't think they had elephant calves at the zoo in those days. I don't remember much about the animals to tell the truth. Mainly I remember how a couple of boys with skateboards stared at Jules on the train. She had just grown breasts—firm things that tented her t-shirt like a couple of smuggled plums—and I remember how she stared out the window, with those long hairless legs neatly tucked beneath her bottom, and how everything in the carriage rattled, it seemed, except for her.

*

Did you know that baby elephants can have more than one mummy? Sometimes, a female cow who is not quite ready to have her own baby, looks after her younger siblings and cousins. The practice is known as allomothering. The female is the allomother.

*

It is standing room only at the elephant enclosure. Molly is up on my shoulders. The calf, his eyes red with fright, cowers beneath the belly of an elderly cow. I'm reminded of Nanna's oak dining table and the long days Jules and I spent playing beneath it. A keeper holds up a loudspeaker.

He informs us that an elephant pregnancy lasts two years. There are gasps from the audience. Mothers mainly. *Imagine that,* they say, and laugh and rub their deflated bellies.

*

"You can use this," Jules said, uncoiling a bandage. "Or take the drugs."

My hands crept up towards my breasts. They were hard and lumpy, like jackfruit.

"You wrap it tight as you can," she said, studying the crepe between her fingers. "Harriet's doula swears by it."

I took the bandage and retreated to the bedroom. Jules had never asked me to express and I had never offered, even though we both knew it would be the best thing for Molly. I suspect it would have undone her: another thing my body could do that hers couldn't.

It took everything not to scream. Milk seeped through the flesh-coloured fabric, creating brown stains above my nipples. It hurt like buggery, as my mother would say, but pain was what I wanted. I'd been asleep for the emergency C-section and had no memory of a labour. I needed to feel the tear of tissues, the gush of blood, the shear of placenta from womb. Because I always thought it should be hideous agonizing to the point of torture—it being the final cleavage of a child from its mother.

*

In the car on the way home I dissect the day's events.
Did you have fun?
What was your favourite part?
Did you enjoy seeing all the animals?
Molly provides monosyllabic answers between long sucks of her dirty thumb. She isn't like me, always looking

in the rear view mirror. She is focused on the road ahead, craning to see what lies around the next bend.

As we park outside her house, Molly sits up straight in her booster seat. Once out, she holds my hand for a millisecond before breaking away to tear down the driveway. I watch her bang on the front door with two fists and stand on tippytoes to reach the handle. I can still feel her hot little hand in mine as I see Julie's long silhouette in the doorway. She can't get inside fast enough. The house swallows her, hungrily.

"Allomother" originally appeared in *The Bridport Prize Anthology 2015*.

Grief

by Pete Fromm

Angie has retreated to our bathroom upstairs, the huge double slipper tub we'd put in when she was pregnant, soaking there now as if she's sailing away, adrift on uncharted currents. I listen for the occasional slosh, some sense of her not having disappeared altogether, but hear only the water draining as she adds more hot, over and over, hours' worth, as if she'll never be warm again. The whole emptied house to myself, the water rushing down the pipes, I do nothing but keep my eyes above any possible trace of Jason, stare at my father's tools, his working tools Angie had mounted in shadow boxes when we cleaned out his place. Antiques all, these things he used every day, able to build or fix anything.

But even this is not safe. When Angie first put them up, Jason couldn't get enough of them. He had me bring them down again and again, let him touch them, come so close to their dangerous edges. Bench planes, edge bevels, mortising chisels, brace and auger bits, all honed to razors, the wood polished with only the oil of my father's skin. He'd taught me their names, tried to train me in their uses, but they remained as foreign in my hands as ever.

Jason begged me to use them, build him a tree house. But after standing side by side beneath our crab apple, my father's carpenter saw dangling useless from my hand, the cape of his Batman jams fluttering in the breeze, he let me off the hook, said he'd really rather have a cave under the house. Bats. A manservant. He took to calling me Alfred.

I shut my eyes, listen for that final pull of the plug, when I'll go up to meet Angie in our bedroom. Week after week of water drying her skin to something she might slough off, I've brought home creams and ointments, prescriptions, hopes I apply with the same incapable hands. She bears the applications, sitting silent on the bed, nude, rolling this way or that, as instructed. I might as well be rubbing marble, polishing the Pieta. When I finish she pulls the sheet over herself and stares at the wall, the ceiling, whatever direction my ministrations have left her. I have tried talking, but we've left that beyond the horizon now, too. The doctors said time, one even rolling out how it heals all wounds. We did not go back for a second session.

The tub, the tools, the lotion, the incredible drag of the clock's second hand, this is what is left to us after the rush, the flowers, the memorials on every corner, the entire city a mortuary, not a soul knowing what to say to any of the twenty families. We with no clearer trail back to the world, no real interest in making the trip.

The reporters are long gone, their headlines, even the tire tracks of their big satellite trucks vanished, the earth risen back up beneath the grass. They won't return until the next, like at Virginia Tech this time, asking those parents how they've dealt with it. Questions as pointless and unanswerable as any ever asked.

The baths, as unable to heal as time, do at least seem to soothe. Angie never says so, but why else? Why spend all your idle hours ensconced in our old tub, the room steamed around you, its memories held as tight and dank as some cloying tropical disease, your skin pruned and puckered as the dead's?

*

It's those questions that draw me upstairs, to the rooms I've avoided ever since the day, a hope of a glimpse of who Angie has become. On one of her rare ventures out, a trip for groceries, the inhuman drive to keep the body alive, I take a book, my reading glasses, and head up like in the old days, when Angie and Jason were off somewhere and I would steal this precious scrap of time alone, no idea how much of it the future held in store.

Originally, Angie had talked about birthing him in the tub—midwives, the water delivery—but we caved to the greater sense of safety of the hospital, the readily available response to any emergency. Once Jason was here, though, safe and sound, strong and healthy, he shrieked with excitement at just the sound of the water filling. We swam him between us, back and forth, diving down, blowing bubbles. We bathed as if we were amphibians, the three of us our own exclusive species. Later we wondered about propriety, a boy of five, six, splashing naked with his parents, but thank God we were able to restrain ourselves from restraining ourselves.

I stand in the bedroom as the water flows, try not to listen, no need to be there to keep anyone safe. I glance at my watch, wonder how much time I'll have before Angie returns. Really, I'd rather not have her find me invading what has become her sole refuge.

I undress, draping my clothes over the rocker still beside the bed, stirring the dust bunnies underneath. Angie had turned the cleaning service away, the cleaning service I'd invited in. A donation they'd said, a gift from caring people across the entire nation. Knifing a single glance my way, Angie was kind, polite, as immovable as stone. No, no, no thank you. Though I did not think it wise, I knew she would give an arm rather than have a single one of his smudges wiped away.

Stepping into the bathroom, I keep my eyes from the opposite door, Jason's room behind it a mausoleum, a place I have not had trace enough of heart left to step into, though I think Angie does go in there sometimes, lies down on his bed, among his things. I could not do it, would never come back out alive. Even out here, there are things, bits of him everywhere, stopping me cold at every turn. Weeks after I'd picked up, put away, tasks once simply routine, I found myself stunned breathless by a fist-sized Batman peeking from between the couch cushions. I staggered, glanced around for him, grasped for bearings, some single compass point to hang from.

I twist the faucet shut and step over the edge, ease myself back, to the left side, Dad's side, as Jason called it, adamant about his protocols.

The heat coils around me and it does feel good, something I have not thought of a single thing since the day, and

I picture Angie here, letting herself sink into that one tiny relief, can feel how puny my hands, my lotions, were after that.

Dutifully, all my motions now only rote, I pick my book from the floor, push my readers high on my nose. I open to the bookmark, slide it toward the front, close those pages over it. I listen for Angie's car, have no idea what the book is, where I am, what's come before, and I read without gaining any clearer picture, without a single word registering as anything beyond ink on a page. I let my arm sag over the tub edge, the book drop to the floor. It is not impossible to imagine the same pose, the chisel-opened vein, the color swirling into the warmth. I let my glasses fall after the book, lean back, wonder about slipping under.

I don't open my eyes until the water has cooled, when I lean forward to pull the plug, the rhythm of Angie's refills in my every move. That's when I see it. The mirror.

For the full past year, Jason has—had—drawn the same crazy smiley face on any surface at hand; frosted windows, snowy windshield, fogged mirrors. His trademark; his arch nemesis, The Joker, everywhere, waiting only to be vanquished. And there it is now, leering out of the steamed mirror, as if Jason's back there himself, smiling in at us, fighting not to laugh. Right there.

I push the plug back into its hole, twist the faucet. More hot pours through the gooseneck, more steam. I cannot believe Angie ever forced herself out of the water. Cannot believe she never told me. I want to take a steamer to every window in the house.

Water hot enough to scald, I only lie back, watch that crazy, goofy smile.

It is the cascade of that steaming rush that hides all other sound, lets Angie open the bathroom door, catch me unaware in her place. I turn at the click of the latch, but she does not even glance to me, looks, instead, straight to her mirror. She smiles, tiny and broken, but, still, closer to anything like what I've seen on her face since the day.

She slips through the door after barely opening it, closes it behind her, keeping in the steam. "You've found him," she whispers.

"Yes," I say.

She doesn't say another word, just steps to the tub, lifts her leg over the lip. Her shoes already kicked off at the back step, she climbs in, her black tights looking the same in the water as out, her Danskin top only clinging a little more tightly to the bones of her, the weight she's shed like a life.

Instead of sliding over to her side, Angie never looks away from the mirror. I open my legs, make a place for her to move into, to ease back, which she does. I wrap her in my arms, and she takes my hands, holds her arms around mine which are around her. Her head touches back against my chest.

"He's here," she says, tightening her grip, and I do not know if she means here with us, in us, or just that ghost of his old outline in the mirror.

I drop my chin to the top of her head, roll so my cheek is against her hair, my face turned away.

Before, seeing it in others—funerals of my parents' friends, the couple across the street after their sullen, hair-in-his-eyes teen drag-raced into the tree—I pictured grief as this shining bright drill bit, like one of my father's, honed and oiled, boring a clean hole straight through the heart. I did not have the experience to go farther than that, to picture, What now? What next? But now I know it as this rust-flecked, bent and twisted auger, grinding through its crooked hole only to wrench back out, dive back in, find some part not yet pierced, boring endlessly, leaving nothing but a sieve for our sorrow to pour through, not near enough left of us to staunch the flow.

And holding Angie alone in our oceanic tub, I feel how it has bored through both of us together, joining us on its auger, Jason's smiley face, which though it will fade no matter our efforts, water-streaked and dust flecked and disappearing, always, always there.

"Grief" originally appeared in *Cream City Review.*

A Good Thing

by Aimee LaBrie

We start the day by going over the list of the dead. I'm new to this job as a transplant coordinator, and I find myself continually shocked by the many ways you can die. It makes me afraid to leave the house in the morning, to cross the street, to walk around in socks. I keep waiting for the story that ends, And then the patient fully recovered and walked out of the hospital with just a slight limp. It never once happens.

The receptionist distributes rolls of all the viable brain dead in the Tri-State area. This week we have two gunshot wounds (one accidental, one self-inflicted), one motor vehicle accident, a suicide via hanging from a NordicTrack machine, and one helmet-less bike messenger flattened by a car on the Walnut Street Bridge.

Alison, a large woman with a hangdog face and tiny hands, talks about her case—a sixteen-year-old boy in North Philadelphia who heard gunshots, stuck his head out his apartment window, and was struck by a stray bullet. The family had lost another son in a shooting two years before.

I consider moving to South Dakota and farming the land. I would raise good-natured beagles and drink only green tea.

Alison met with the dead boy's family for over two hours while they argued back and forth about what the boy would have wanted. Finally, the patient herniated and was declared brain dead. The family consented to donate all but his corneas.

"What did we learn from this case?" asks Andrew Clarke. He's the director. He has a rugged, pockmarked face and blue eyes. I imagine he'd be excellent in bed, persuasive and reassuring at the same time.

Alison looks at the ceiling. She's been at the hospital for twenty-four hours straight. There are dark circles under her eyes; traces of prettiness swim in the tired lines of her face. "We learned to stall the family until the patient throws a clot," she says.

We clap. I'm grateful for all of it—these people who make jokes and speak inappropriately so that we can get up and do this again the next day.

Training lasts two months.

Words and phrases we're taught not to use when dealing with the donor family: harvest, excision, cadaver, organ procurement, dead as a doornail.

Words we do use: saving the lives of others, donation, transplant, every form of to give. We talk about the patient in the past tense—What would she have wanted?—even as the blip of the heart monitor persists in the background.

We learn to compartmentalize our feelings. I picture giant pieces of luggage stuffed with body parts: a bowling bag with a head in it, a trunk holding a torso, a golf bag filled with legs.

Before we face real people, we practice the rhetoric of donation through role-play. One day I'm a mother of two who has lost her husband in a car crash late at night on I-95. I get carried away as the grieving widow, sobbing and exclaiming, "But he was so young!"

My partner, Jesse, pats me on the back with his fat, soft hands. "There, there," he says.

The instructor, a tall man with bangs, advises us to take a five-minute break. He comes over and asks if I'm OK. "You were very convincing," he says. I thank him. He asks if I can do it again for the next group of trainees. Of course. Of course I can.

We take numerous classes: Empathetic Listening, Donor Management, Donation after Cardiac Death, Donors without Heartbeats, and Ways People Die in the Bathroom. "You don't want to know," I tell my boyfriend later.

We're sitting in the living room in the dark watching cars blow up in an action-packed thriller involving a foreign invasion. He turns down the volume. "Let me guess. You fall off the toilet and hit your head, right? You slip in the shower?"

Yes, those are some of the ways. I don't mention the others.

A newborn is thrown into a Porta-Potty by his anxious young mother.

A guy ODs over a urinal at Locust Bar his first time shooting up.

A woman falls backward through a glass shower door because the water is too hot.

A man cuts an artery shaving.

He says, "Would you rather watch a movie with kitties in it?"

I say, "Yes, please," and he changes the channel to Animal Planet. But what I really want is for him to keep asking me questions.

Later that week I'm at my boyfriend's end-of-summer work party, stuck in a group of accountants who think that wearing a cartoon tie makes them whimsical. Most are drinking martinis.

I'm standing at the edge of a small knot of them when a tall woman with impossibly shiny hair turns to me. "And what do you do?" she asks.

I tell her I'm into organs. At first, she thinks that means I play an instrument, so I begin with the most recent story: a family on vacation from China whose five-year-old son fell off the edge of the LOVE sculpture while his dad was taking a photo. They stare at me like I'm a monster. Maybe I am. I can't get enough of this stuff. I try to explain that in every story, no matter how ghastly, something funny happens, or something odd.

"Yes, it's hilarious that their child died," spits the lady with the glowing hair.

"Not that. The odd/funny part was what the father said after the coordinator explained brain death to him. He didn't speak English very well, and he nodded and nodded and then said, 'Yes, yes, I get it. We want brain transplant!'" No one laughs. "I didn't mean funny like, funny ha-ha; I meant funny like, awful funny."

I want to tell them that you have to talk about it this way; otherwise, you'd lie down on the floor and never get up.

Much later, after I've had my fourth glass of chardonnay and I'm finishing up a story about a girl whose parents refused to donate because they thought their daughter would snap out of it, a man with thick sideburns and an upturned nose announces, "Well, I for one don't want some guy letting me die so they can transplant my organs. No, thank you! That's what they do. They just take everything, before you're even dead."

The other guests nod or stare into their drinks.

They know about organ donation from TV shows like ER or Dateline—the transplant recipient who begins to act like the dead donor, the doctor paid off to remove the kidney of a perfectly healthy kid, the boy who receives a baboon heart. I know this, and yet I still can't quite believe it—I can't believe they believe it. "Yes, we want every last thing," I say. "Even your eyeballs." I fish the olive out of his drink and pop it into my mouth. "Mmm. Tasty."

My boyfriend pulls me into the kitchen. "Hey, listen, maybe you should switch topics. You know, try talking about the weather. And not about how it relates to a fatal car accident, if you can help it." He gives me a tight, angry smile.

The hostess enters the room and sees that we're busy hating each other. She says, "Whoopsie daisy!" and swivels away on her heels.

"Maybe we should make up conversation topics on index cards," I suggest, barely slurring, "and you can hand them to me as the evening goes on."

"Great idea." He takes my arm and steers me out the door, his grip hard against my elbow. Good, I think. Maybe tomorrow there'll be a bruise.

I want to be more giving to him. I leave him little Sticky Notes in the medicine cabinet. Don't forget your umbrella. Looks like rain. Or 2 good 2 B 4 gotten. He doesn't mention them. I want to give him something of myself: my eyes, my fingers, my heart. Instead, I mop the bathroom floor and check out books for him from the library, mostly about the American Revolution.

After my last day of training, I present him with a bicycle helmet. "Just wear it." He shakes his head. "Hey, try not to worry about your hair. Worry about your brain being splattered on the sidewalk outside of a Starbucks. Think how embarrassing that would be." I strap the helmet on my own head. "Look, look—you'll be the envy of all of your friends." I try to explain that he has no idea how dangerous the world can be. Bricks fall from the sky. Ice is slippery. You can be at a bar having a nice conversation, then say the wrong thing, and some burly construction worker can hit you over the head with a Heineken bottle. "These are matters of life and death. You should pay attention."

He says, "You were happier when you were an RN at that doctor's office. Remember those days? Remember when you always wanted to take my temperature?" At one time in our relationship this would've been a come-on. Now he gives me a look like I'm a defective purchase he wants to return. "I think I liked you better then."

I lie on the floor in front of him, still wearing the helmet. "I think I liked me better then, too."

He turns on the TV, to a rerun of Law & Order: Special Victims Unit, and politely asks me to move.

At our work Halloween party I count one Terri Schiavo, two blood bank operators with fake blood splattering their clothes, several ghosts, a few zombies, three vampires, and a cat. We're a scary bunch. My boyfriend has consented to go with me—a rare occasion. I parade him around the room, introducing him proudly as if to say, Look, look, this is the person who tolerates me!

He's dressed as a Holstein cow—the same costume he's worn for two years running. I go as the Bride of Frankenstein. We stand by the punch bowl spiked with vodka. I've made a mental list of conversational topics to use with him—ones that don't involve blood thinner or dead children.

We all drink too much and get swept away by the karaoke. Andrew, the director—dressed as a caveman with a single, thick eyebrow drawn across his forehead—croons "Living on a Prayer." His eyes are squeezed shut with sincerity. It's the same look he bears when speaking to families, and the expression I imagine him wearing during sex.

I realize I'm staring at Andrew and turn instead to my boyfriend. His cow horns are crooked. I straighten them. "I find you udderly attractive," I say, knowing it sounds unconvincing.

He gives me a side hug.

I'll go on at least sixteen cases with a seasoned coordinator before I'm set free to convince families on my own. My first time out, I'm paired with Bryan.

The case is an eight-month-old girl whose mother accidentally left the baby carrier on top of the family SUV, then backed out of the driveway, still talking to the child she thought she'd clicked into the car seat. Halfway down the block she braked at a stop sign and heard a thump. She assumed at first that a neighbor's garbage can had tipped over. Then the truth of what occurred rose with appalling certainty in her throat.

You think this story is an urban legend; you've heard it before, or something similar. But here's the thing: it really happened. It happens and worse: a drunk father who accidentally runs over his son with his ATV, a hunter who mistakes his brother for a stag, a girl whose hits her twin sister in the head with a lacrosse ball.

While we're waiting for the neurologist to declare the baby brain dead, another call comes in on Bryan's Blackberry. Thirty-four-year-old Caucasian male, hit by a car while biking to work. I wonder how I would feel if it turned out to be my boyfriend. I find myself blushing at the thought. How selfish I am. Why must everything relate back to me? And yet, I imagine the funeral scene: me as the stoic girlfriend, his family caving under the grief. I try to work myself into tears, as I was able to do in training, but can't seem to muster up the correct emotion.

And of course it's not him. It's someone else's boyfriend, someone who's not as lucky as me.

After the baby is pronounced, Bryan and I go into the waiting room, where the father paces. The mother, hysterical, has been heavily sedated. We talk to the father about donation. He nods and looks back and forth between our faces with a look of complete bafflement. "Yes," he says when we're finished. "Yes, if she can save another baby, then yes. Do whatever you need to do."

He wants something good to come out of this tragedy—anything, anything, one good thing.

The baby has a full head of black curls like her dad. Her eyes are shut and rimmed with blue bruises. She resembles a baby panda bear. She is impossibly small and pale and I want to wrap her up and hide her in my coat, take her home with me, and pray for a miracle.

Initially we're hopeful. The doctors work hard to keep her heart beating so she can be a donor, so we can give the family something. They pump her body full of blood thinner to maintain her for the operating room. But she arrests. All her organs become toxic, unusable, worthless.

And she dies and no one is saved and my head empties of reason. The father shakes my hand with a blank look on his face. It will take some time for the truth to sink in.

I walk all the way home in my sensible black heels, hoping for blisters as penance for being one of the living, for not having to survive without someone I love.

I go into the house, where my boyfriend is sitting at the kitchen table doing a crossword puzzle. He's wearing his glasses, which reminds me of when we first met. He brought his mom into the doctor's office because she couldn't stop hiccupping. He wore his glasses then, too, and I thought, What a sweet guy. He loves his mother. He looks up. "How did it go?"

"We lost the baby," I tell him.

"Well, have you tried looking under the sofa?" He glances back to his puzzle.

I open my mouth to tell him what happened and then shut it again.

I go upstairs. He's plugged in the radio again over the bathroom sink, just a few feet from the tub. I unplug it, wind the cord around the center, and stow it in the closet behind a mountain of towels.

I lie on our bed, hands on either side of my body like a dead person. I begin listing parts of the anatomy, beginning with the letter a and working my way down the alphabet: aorta, bronchial tube, cranium, duodenum. This is how I distract myself from thinking about what I should do.

And then, just in time for Christmas, it's my turn to go on a case alone. They give me a black beeper. I might be called once on the shift, twice, three times, or never. The day burns bright with just a slight chance of snow. I pray this means no one will die today. Tomorrow, OK. But please not today.

My boyfriend has called in sick to work. He perches on the sofa in his droopy gray jogging pants, playing a video game that requires him to shoot people with a semiautomatic machine gun and drive a sports car. I sit next to him. "What's the point of this game?" I ask.

He can't answer because he's concentrating, speeding down a twisting highway in Southern California. He's explained to me that the game is an exact replica of Los Angeles and the outlying areas, down to each building and street. Just like real life.

I nudge him with my foot. "How do you win?"

"Damn it!" We watch his car careen off a cliff and plunge into the water. Seconds later his man surfaces, unharmed, and begins swimming toward shore. "You don't win."

"Then why do you play?" I don't state the obvious: that his video game hero would've been an organ donor a hundred times over by now—because at some point, my God, I have to shut up.

"It's a rush." This is what he wants our life to be like—one long, fun-filled adventure after another with no real casualties.

The beeper goes off an hour later.

I call the office. Marla, the receptionist, gives me the details. Couple involved in a car accident, sideswiped by a truck whose driver had been awake all night trying to make a noon delivery to New York. The husband has superficial cuts on his neck and chest. Doctors are working to save the wife, but she has an internal bleed. I ask the questions I think I'm supposed to ask while putting on my hat and shoes. I attempt to zipper my coat and realize my hands are shaking.

Marla tells me to call if I don't think I can handle it and she'll send in another coordinator. She tells me I'll be fine. This is my first conversation with her, and she's managed to calm me down in a way I know my boyfriend never could.

"Leave the light on for me," I tell him. He nods. I waver by the front door. "Good-bye, then."

"Good—" he begins, but stops as his car plummets off yet another cliff.

I see the truck driver who killed the woman, sitting in the waiting room. He's a mammoth of a man in red flannel, a John Deere cap tucked back on his head. His eyes are wide, and his face is a picture of raw disbelief. When he sees me, he stands, taking off his hat.

"I didn't mean it," he says.

"I know," I say.

The rush of people swooshes around us—nurses, a little boy wailing, families arguing. A TV mounted near the ceiling broadcasts close-up after close-up of beautiful soap opera actors, their artful faces bearing a whole range of recognizable expressions: sadness, joy, jealousy, triumph, fear.

I ask a nurse if she can find an open bed for the trucker, so that he can lie down for a while. She says OK and he follows her obediently, like a large child.

The surgeon greets me as I walk into the ICU. He's an older man with graying hair and deep-set brown eyes. I'm in luck: he's one of the good doctors, one who's treated transplant recipients in the past, not one who calls us "the death squad."

He explains the situation. No hope of survival for the wife. She hasn't taken a breath on her own in two hours and has failed two apnea tests. The CAT scan shows no cerebral blood flow. I nod. "OK, OK."

He knows it's my first solo case. "You can handle it," he says.

I take a deep breath and go into the patient's room. The husband sits beside her bed. My training has taught me that the dead look dead. They don't appear kind of dead or somewhat dead. Even as their chests rise and fall because of the ventilator, there's something missing in them.

The woman's dark hair is pulled off her face with a headband. Around the room her family and friends have left flowers, balloons, stuffed animals, as if she were a kid having her tonsils out. One of her eyes is half open. If I pulled up the lid, I'd see the pupil blown out, filling the white. In slide presentations during training, it looked like

146

something from a scary movie—the eye of death, one might say, if one were given to such dramatizations. Her other eye has been covered by a white bandage, giving her a slightly jaunty air.

The husband is tall and handsome with stubble on his chin. He's been told that there's no chance of recovery, no miracle on its way. He's seen the nurse put a cotton swab to his wife's eye and watched as it didn't blink or move. "We were only married for a year," he tells me. "We just moved into a new house. We haven't even hung up the pictures yet."

"I'm sorry." Instead of dispensing the platitudes we've been taught (You can give the gift of life! It's your time to make a difference. One dead wife equals seven others saved!), I listen to him. I listen to him talk about his wife, Lena, for a long time. They met in a dive bar in Northern Liberties. He thought she'd be a one-night stand, but he stayed that night, and the next, and the next, and then he moved in his stereo and that was it. They were married in Hawaii by a priest with a lisp. They have a fat golden retriever named Jack. He pauses, staring off toward the wall. His eyes are clear and blue. "How am I going to break the news to Jack?" he says. His gaze turns to me. "Maybe I should tell him to sit first?" His laughter comes out in a burst.

I say, "Maybe you should remind him that he's a good boy?" We're both laughing. It's hysterical, this laughter, and a blessing.

The doctor hovers in the doorway. It's time to go. I ask the husband if there's anything he wants to do before we take her to the operating room.

He doesn't hesitate. "Could you find me a brush or a comb? Her hair is a mess. She would hate that." I get him a brush. We set her headband on the dresser beside the bed. I hold her so that he can reach the back of her head. He brushes her hair with careful, clumsy strokes.

We don't talk about donation. The husband has already consented. I don't have to convince him of anything. He knows what she would have wanted. He knows what she would have said.

When he's finished, he puts her headband back on. I remain quiet, though I know they'll remove it in the operating room. "You're doing a good thing," I tell him.

He nods and I leave him alone for a moment, not because I'm generous but because I can't stand to watch them say good-bye.

I follow the transplant recovery team into the OR. The woman has become "the body," "the chest," no longer the person, the wife, Lena Dixon. They wrap her in clear plastic, cocooning her. The nurse swabs her with iodine and the room fills with the smell of it.

The surgeon picks up a scalpel. His eyes flicker to me as if checking whether I'm OK. I'm OK. Everything is a-OK. He makes a long incision from throat to stomach. Another doctor cracks open the sternum. The chest bone is difficult to break; sometimes they have to use a saw. The surgeon snips the aortic valve, delicately, his pinky raised, and then I see it. It's bigger than I thought it would be—twice the size of my fist. Not red, not beautiful. A purple and black muscle, a wonderful and horrible thing, still beating.

The rest of the transplant surgeons do what they need to do. The heart will be placed in a red cooler and flown via helicopter to a different hospital where another family waits. The lungs are trickier and may not be usable. The liver might go to a local woman, the kidneys to two other people. Skin tissue for burn victims. Corneas for a blind person. One life to save seven others.

It's a good thing. It's a good thing. It's a good thing. I repeat this to myself while the nurse sews the empty body closed with neat black stitches.

It's 4 A.M. when I stumble through the hospital's automatic doors. My legs tremble from standing for so long. The parking lot is deserted, the moon just beginning to fade as streaks of orange and purple flood across the sky. The start of another beautiful day.

The porch light is off, which shouldn't matter really since it's already dawn. I fumble with the keys for a long time before I unlock the front door.

I pull off my shoes and notice a hole in my tights. This makes me think again of the black threads across Lena Dixon's skin, how the nurse stitched her up as though it were a normal procedure, and not the end of something.

I drag myself upstairs to the bedroom and stand over the sleeping shape of my boyfriend. His arm is thrown up over his head as if to shield himself from an attack. He seems younger; in sleep he doesn't have to arrange his face in any particular way to prepare for what I might say next.

He was dear to me once. At least, I think he was.

In training we learned the many reasons people say no. They say no because they look at the body and can't believe their son, daughter, husband, wife, brother, sister won't snap out of it. They say no because they understand that doctors make mistakes, or because they hear the word coma

149

and believe there's a chance their loved one can be saved. Because they still have hope. They say no because they met someone who knows someone whose brother was in a terrible car wreck but made a slow recovery and is now bagging groceries at the local supermarket. They say no because they can't bear that their son's dog will outlive their son. They say no because they raised this child, fell in love with this face, remember with clarity how he used to move around in space, his habit of gesturing with his hands when telling a story. They say no because to say yes would mean accepting death.

I sit at the kitchen table and make a list. The sun creeps across the floor as I write.

Replace the tangle of cords beneath your computer. Buy new batteries for the smoke alarm. Sidewalk salt for when it's icy. A waterproof radio for the bathroom. Duck-shaped stickies for the bottom of the tub ... I write until my hand aches; this is the last good thing I can do before I leave.

"A Good Thing" originally appeared in *Zoetrope: All-Story*, where it won the journal's annual short fiction contest.

Crowned

by Marjorie Maddox

Pumpkin, apple, sorghum, blueberry—I do all the festivals. Judge giant pies the size of wading pools. Win goldfish religiously. Sip milkshakes as thick as all my wishes. At each one, I am the queen, a half-wave to the left, a half-wave to the right, riding on a shiny John Deere or a customized Cadillac while my court follows on Harleys or streamered pick-ups. What does the rest of my life matter when I have a basket of berries, when 4-H kids stand on their tiptoes and point at my crown?

You don't have to be television-pretty. I am the preacher's kid and have twenty-three freckles on my face, one for each of my talents, my daddy says. I think it's for the times we'll move in and out of duplexes, refurbished garages, or a parsonage in need of electricity and paint. We arrive well before the voting when any new girl is cute enough and a minister's someone important, his wife voted to every committee.

But there's only Daddy and I and the empty slots for Dog-Sled or Quilting Festival Queen. My hair is long, shiny, uncut. Daddy says that's the crown of any girl, that and a Christian way of being, honest-like and full of thankyou's. I catch on quick, remember how Mama was before the baby that took them both. It wasn't Jesus that did it. He let his mama live. Saved her one of the biggest crowns in heaven. My mama has one too, I'm sure—sparkled as sweetness. But I don't think the baby's there, seeing what she did by trying to be born too quickly. She should have waited her turn.

Daddy and I know about taking turns. When he sees someone at the convenience store, scowling as he sorts through the Shop Mart guides, Daddy says to me, "This one is yours. Turn on that pretty smile and tell him about Jesus." When he sees a new bank teller or the secretary at the town insurance company, he says, "This one is mine" and smiles big as eternity. Then he gives her directions to church and our number. We know what's to be done. If you're not nice, there's nobody to fill the pews. It's the job, and we work quickly. "There's only so many days before Jesus comes back," Daddy says each time he sees a new clerk at the Coastal Mart.

Time keeps moving, and people move with it. Knowing that makes it easy. People will wave goodbye in a few months anyway no matter what. The first Sunday they return all our smiles. The next Sunday, too. The months after that, their smiles loosen a bit each time they shut the church door and walk back to their own lives. I know because of what my daddy knows: how their pity reminds them of their own pain, and their pain embarrasses them.

At first, they bring Daddy's favorite casseroles, though I cook just fine. Next, they bring stories of their mothers and their own losses, hidden inside bites of upside-down cake. Finally, they forget about us and our lives. They want us to forget about theirs. They look away, trying to erase their calls at midnight, their shaky voices, and the lives they don't put on parade. I watch them during my solos of "When the Saints Come Marching In." By the last notes, they don't remember my festival crown. They see instead my father's eyes and the slant of his nose; they remember the words he's heard.

I hear some of them, too, though I'm not supposed to. What can I do when Sally Moore's mother arrives red-eyed on the doorstep, a bruise tattooing her arm? She needs my daddy to listen, so I go for the ice. Her words heave between a chorus of sobs. "It's only sometimes," she says, her voice not believing itself. When my daddy's strong arm goes around her, she calms a bit, but keeps talking. Her life comes out of her lips: how her own daddy was, where she'd lived. She was even a festival queen like me, but only once. My own breath comes fast as I wait for her to finish the hard part. She says what has been stuck inside too long: the way she got the baby before she should have. How she married quick, without even a proper dress or a daddy who would give her away. It's then my daddy whispers Bible verses in her ear, the way he did to me when I was a little girl. When I look down, the ice is dripping tiny puddles at my feet. I let it dry up by itself and head to the bedroom.

The next week the plant closes, and Bob Harker sobs on Daddy's shoulder right in the middle of the hardware store. I have the basket with all the stuff we're buying: a new roll of screen for the backdoor to keep the flies out, more oil for the squeaky door hinge that wakes me up each time Daddy has to go out at night. Standing in line with some rope, Mr. Harker sees Daddy and his eyes well up. Then the crying starts. Loud. Even Julie, the cash register girl, knows to look away. Daddy takes him by the shoulder and walks him over by the electric saws where no one else is. They're gone long enough for me to go up and down most of the aisles three times. Then I just sit up front by the Child Safety display and work on my memory verses. When I get done with that, I practice my festival speech, quiet-like so no one can hear. I even practice the hand gestures, imagining the audience. At the end, I look up, thinking how light the new crown will feel.

It's almost closing time when Daddy and Mr. Harker come out. The rope's gone. Instead, Daddy's got us a new welcome mat and holds it up to show me. He shakes Mr. Harker's hand, as if nothing's happened; says he'll see him at church.

We're a team like that, Daddy and I. We're the 1 + 1 = 2 for Noah's ark. We're a right foot and a left foot to march around Jericho. We're the hands to pick the wheat for the holy harvest. So when Freddy Schmidt smashes the family car into the front of Greeley's Garage six hours before Sunday School, we both go. It's just across the street and down a bit, and the ambulance sirens blast through the walls of our tiny house and into the one bedroom. Daddy's up first, tugging on some shorts and a WWJD T-shirt. Quick, like that; then he's out the door. I'm right behind him with some shorts over my nightie. No time for a bra.

When we get there, the ambulance guys are prying Freddy out of the Buick. He's dazed and bleeding across his forehead, Jesus-style. The garage storefront is a mess. Glass everywhere. The car is propped up like those modern sculptures they have at the museums, the front end smashed in like a flattened milk carton. One tire is still spinning. A poster that reads "Change Your Oil. It's Sooner Than You Think" hangs crookedly from what's left of the one wall. There's no alarm, this being a small town, but the neighbors have all come out from across the street and stare at the wreck. They're comparing raising-kid stories, I think. Daddy waves at them, then holds his praying hands up high. The ambulance lights flash across his fingers. It's then I think Freddy looks at me, just for a second, smiling as they carry him off on the stretcher.

We get to the hospital even before his parents, and Daddy puts me on door watch. It's only a few minutes before the Schmidts come rounding the corner in the other car, the one mostly she uses, a rusted-out Toyota. Mr. Schmidt is driving too fast (who wouldn't?), but the parking lot is pretty empty, so there's lots of space to make up for the bad turns and the speed. He parks crooked, taking up two spaces, and they're out and running in. She's got on a nightgown and shorts like I do; he's dressed like Daddy, but with a Harley T-shirt. They almost don't see me, but I know enough to run with them, pointing toward a doctor and Daddy. Just like on TV, only better. My daddy's there for Mrs. Schmidt to wrap her arms around. She's crying hysterically and even reaches for my hand twice. It's a good morning, considering. Freddy ends up OK, and Daddy takes me out to Perkins before Sunday School. I get hash browns, pancakes, and scrambled eggs. The waitress recognizes me from my picture in the paper.

*

In every town, that's how it starts. In the next weeks, grateful choruses of Amen's will punctuate the sermons. They'll be Sunday supper invitations, strong handshakes, and kisses on the cheek. What follows are the shopping lists jotted on the back of bulletins, the kids-have-a-cold excuses, and the rushed goodbyes. After that, the complaints: sermons too long, budget too high, attendance too low, building too cold.

So before all that, I try to remember the parades. I hold the day in my head like a prayer and deeply inhale the peanut-greasy-fries-caramel-apple smell that circles everyone in town halo-style. I look and see the not-yet familiar faces, unscrubbed for Sunday but breaking with the same otherworldliness that hymns give, a sudden note of joy that takes you from a job you hate and lets you breathe in and out without thinking. The kids are happy and kiss their mothers. The parents hold hands. Most of them recognize me and wave. Like my daddy, I am up front, where everybody looks. I think my crown shimmers like the heavenly ones.

It's the same in every town, wherever we go. The parade rides down whatever the largest street is, past whatever church has hired Daddy, and up toward some rented Ferris wheel where chips of rust float like confetti out over the game barkers. Someone will offer to win me a giant teddy bear or a new Bible, but I'll be listening to the marching band's last song—brash and off-key—the town fire engines shrieking their sirens, prophesying, as I do, what is coming. Because I know.

Daddy says talent is God-given, but I know it's just memorizing the patterns, the important dates, the order and kinds of parades, and what to do when it rains. I can sing and dance OK. I can ride a unicycle without breaking my leg. I can even do three back flips in a row, but that's not what wins me my crown. I know what people want by looking at them. I know who will let out the pain, who will want someone else to feel it. They see a motherless girl and they think, "She knows." They see a man without a wife, and they think, "He knows." It's in their eyes just when they finish smiling hello. It's in what's left of their voices after they shake hands, like an aftertaste that won't go away. That's how it was with Miss Samuels—even before she brought the pies wrapped up with a ribbon.

And the others, the ones who already have kids, they think I am more grateful than their own children. Maybe I am. I have less time and take what I can. I sing "Danny Boy" for Mrs. McCleary, recite the twenty-third Psalm for Joe Johnston, and tap dance "Yankee Doodle Dandy" for old Mr. Abernathy. "What a lovely girl," they say, then listen closely to my daddy's sermons, his voice as earnest as a carnival boy hawking frozen bananas, but kinder.

I want them to listen, but not closely. Not enough to repent. When they repent, they only do so half-heartedly, even when they mean it at the time. They walk down that aisle at the altar call and want to be different. When they walk back, they think they are. When they walk out the big double doors, a little wears off, but not much. When they walk back for Wednesday service, they're sure they've got it down, but then they hear Daddy's soft voice. They remember something they didn't do that they should have or something they shouldn't have done that they did, and they walk down the aisle again. The next week it's a little harder and a little harder still after that.

By the time five Sundays have passed, Mrs. Moore has another bruise, only this time just her eyes say something. Part of what they say is shame. Her husband is an elder. They always are. His eyes say embarrassed. They say, forget what you know.

That's what my eyes used to say every time the congregation decided we knew too much. What the people told us was different: They didn't have enough to pay, or Daddy's sermons weren't good enough, or they got a full-time pastor, one with a wife and five girls, all pretty. These days, my eyes aren't embarrassed. There's always another town, another festival, or another parade with unfamiliar faces. At least that's what I tell myself each night when I'm supposed to be saying my prayers.

This month it's Millville and the Strawberry Festival. The people have different names, but inside they're mostly the same. We arrive on a Thursday in May—after the Coal Festival in Blossburg and before the Corn Festival in wherever we end up next. By the next Tuesday, after Daddy's sweet-voice sermon and my solo on Sunday, I am nominated and out back of the Town Hall being questioned by the judges. It's the first thing in the morning. My freckles are a plus. In the sun, my hair looks a little red, so I'm a natural for the part. The church is a festival sponsor, though most of its girls are too young or too old. Wholesome is what this group wants, a good example for its youth.

After a dozen or so towns, I know the part. I wear a handsewn blouse from the last town's ladies' circle, sky blue the color of innocence with a large strawberry for each collar. The shirt flattens my breasts and falls halfway down my calf-length skirt. It's the right choice. I quote a poem from a Hallmark Mother's Day card. Then, to the tune of "We Gather Together," I trill a song about the town. It's a quick revision to what I performed four towns back. I hold out the last notes long and loud, then smile with all my teeth. The men look at their wives for their reactions. The women nod approvingly.

When the first weekend in June rolls around, Daddy is still the man up front in the pulpit. I am still the new festival queen. We are riding high, getting ready for my crown. Three new families have joined the church. The offering is up. Crops are good. We've had supper invitations each week, twice from Miss Samuels, who, she reminds us again though we don't need telling, makes the best pies in town.

Daddy is preaching on the fruits of the Spirit, and the older ladies are trying to identify who has what gift. Three of the younger girls are my court; they smile like junior bridesmaids and wear their hair like mine, a braid twirled into a loose bun, like a hat slipped to the back of the head. One of the girl's grandmother makes us matching red-gingham dresses with a sash the color of vines.

In the parade, we're up front—where we should be. This time, Daddy, the girls, and I all ride in the same car: a convertible, maroon Thunderbird from Walter's backyard mechanic shop. One of the doors is blue and rusting. There are crepe-paper leaves draped across the sides. The girls are scrunched together in the back like triplets, and I ride up front with Daddy, who turns the key as if he's young again and heading out on his honeymoon. My winner's banner is tight and, because it's hot, the ribbon sticks a bit at my shoulder. The *S* in Strawberry Queen is partly gone and looks like a backwards *c*. I don't mind.

I've clipped the gold-sprayed crown in place with bobby pins, but if I wave too vigorously, it tips a bit, back and forth. I try to keep my head straight, yet there's too much to see. The booths are lined up outside the church and down the street: strawberry ice cream, strawberry shortcake, strawberry cupcakes in ice-cream cones, strawberry pudding, strawberry soda, strawberry CRÊPES. There's a booth for weaving strawberry placemats and one selling strawberry air freshener. A woman on the corner, not a churchgoer, holds up strawberry pinwheels and lets them spin in the wind.

Daddy drives us past slowly. I breathe in the redness, pick out faces in the crowded patch of near-strangers. Then there are the others, the ones who've told us too much. They wave, too.

The high school band blasts "In the Good Old Summertime," hold their heads high, and bounce their knees up to their chests. Just behind us, six- and seven-year-olds, dressed like strawberries, do cartwheels and flips for the clapping bystanders. It's time for me to throw candy, so I reach in one of my baskets and pull out strawberry taffy, each piece attached to a pink curl of paper with a different fruit of the Spirit and a Bible reference penned in neat calligraphy. A crowned missionary, I'm spreading the Word!

Then Daddy turns the wheel and heads us to the town square, where a merry-go-round twirls its fantasy promises in the middle of a large circle of park benches. I want doves, but they've flown away. A few sparrows twitter in their place, trying to keep tune with the pretend ponies. At the stand next to the strawberry fritters, past the Tunnel of Love and Monsters Scare Shack, Miss Samuels stands outside her red-checkered booth with her pies stacked neatly inside, away from the heat. Her sign is in large, curvy calligraphy, but she's standing so I can't see the price. A single spot of strawberry filling dots her lower lip. When she looks at my daddy, her eyes hold the light, the same way the candles shine in them during Holy Communion. And she is waiting to tell him her life.

I start singing "A Bicycle Built for Two" for my daddy, so he'll look at me instead, but it's too late. He is already waving at Miss Samuels, his left hand high in the air. He forgets he's a preacher. By the time he glances toward me, he's at the corner and takes the turn—even at slow speed—a bit too sharply, just enough so the girls in back say, "Whoa!" The car nudges up against the curb, and I have to steady my crown. When he looks again at me, his face is different. His eyes are a question. For a moment, I forget the sound of his voice. Without his striped tie and white shirt, he's just a regular dad, so I keep my face ahead and smile, looking toward the horizon where I'm sure the next town is hiding, ready to be found, like a strawberry too long in the sun.

"Crowned" orginally appeared in *Dirt: An Anthology* (The New Yinzer Press) and *What She Was Saying* (Fomite Press).

The Complications of Friendship
by Randi Miller

The Loyalist

Last year, at the school picnic, she was the only friend who refused to talk to your ex-husband's girlfriend—the woman with whom he was sleeping before he walked out of your life—while everyone else carried on as if the pair had been high school sweethearts. She's also the only friend who—in front of the ladies on Ladies Night Out—asked the head of the PTA which yard sale she'd bought her sweater at, in response to the jab that the centerpieces you'd arranged for the picnic lacked pizzazz.

Now, she tells you everything. Toe-to-toe, you sit separated by only a wedge of table and the coffee-scented steam that billows between you. She's raging about Angela Cromwell, a mutual acquaintance who cornered her husband at a party last night. You weren't there, so detail by detail she serves up specifics about Angie's behavior: the schoolgirl giggles at his half-funny jokes, the martini-free hand finding its way to the hump of his bicep. You've known Angie for two years, and have come to admire her level-headedness. You also know Angie is happily married, so the words your friend piles up don't stack neatly in your mind.

"Maybe you're misreading," you say, like a question. "Wasn't her husband at the party too?"

"He was totally unfazed!" your friend says, tossing up her hands in the space between you. Her yellow hair, loosely twisted and clipped, is set in a mound too heavy for her head. Strands come loose and fall in her eyes. "I wouldn't be surprised if they were swingers!" she adds.

She's told you of other, similar episodes regarding Angie's behavior, though you've attended parties together and have never witnessed them yourself. You want to say something supportive, but you are by nature a logical person, so instead you pick your words like blossoms, delicately, skillfully.

"Did anyone say anything?" You hope to sound more incredulous than skeptical.

"People never do," she says, crossing her arms.

Her sincerity is unquestionable, though her interpretations are not. She is still convinced her daughter would have played Dorothy in The Wizard of Oz, if the other child's parents hadn't donated money to the school's Annual Fund. To this day, her conviction remains resolute, so you've stopped mentioning that the other girl has the vocal range of Mariah Carey.

"We need to set that home-wrecker straight," your friend says, leaning forward.

"Let me think," you say, looking down at your latte.

You want to be on her side. If the situation were re-versed, she would be on yours in a heartbeat.

The Soul Sister

She grew up two doors down from you on the same sleepy street, and pretended it was normal when your mother spent three hours lining up vacuum tracks on the orange shag. You dared each other to ring Jay Blundell's doorbell then hid behind the maples to glimpse his bad-boy eyes. Every time you went to the mall, salesclerks asked if you were sisters.

Today is the biggest job you've landed since launching your event planning company, which was one of the first things you did after becoming a single mom. With twenty minutes until the luncheon begins, you set out nametags, straighten silverware, and ask your employee to change a stained tablecloth.

"Where's your friend with those gift bags?" your em-ployee asks, and mumbles something like, "This is ridicu-lous."

"On her way," you say, with more confidence than you feel.

You check your phone and look to the doorway, hoping to spot that heart-shaped face you've envied since third grade. You knew when you hired your oldest friend that it might not be the smartest move, but you also knew she was desperate for work and was saving to go to night school. She has known you long enough to know you're a punctual person who takes commitments seriously. She also knows the significance of today because you reminded her yesterday, when you discussed the final seating plan and she promised to be on time. Twice you've lectured her on the importance of promptness. Both times she swore it wouldn't happen again. Both times she added how lost she'd be if you hadn't given her this job.

If today goes well the two-year contract could pay for a full year of childcare, and would likely lead to enough new business to warrant an actual bookkeeper. You pinch the ache between your eyes and try not to think about implications. Instead you remember the strawberry milkshake your friend poured on Paul Charney's car when she caught him humping Amy Walters in his front seat at the drive-in. It was the movie he had promised to take you to, right after you finally slept with him.

As your employee adjusts the tablecloth to hang perfectly straight, you continue to glance at the doorway in which your friend is not standing. Your phone dings. She'll be there in an hour. In an hour the event will be just about over. You told her this yesterday too.

She never told you about the milkshake. You heard it from Amy Walters.

The Lifestyler

She was the first person to invite your family out for dinner when you were new in town. She recommended her pediatrician, her accountant, and her hairstylist, who are now your pediatrician, your accountant, and your hairstylist. Between book club and cooking group you see each other at least twice a month, and back when you were married your husbands rode bikes together Saturday mornings.

These days, your sons attend different schools, but often beg for play-dates. You watch her children now and then—sometimes you offer, other times she asks—and though you're now working and it's occasionally inconvenient, you figure it out because that's what friends do. Every time she picks her children up, she thanks you profusely and gives you a loose hug. Her skin smells of lavender, with traces of rubbing alcohol.

One day you ask if you can drop off your son an hour earlier than planned; you're already in her neighborhood because you've dropped your daughter nearby, and the bank across town has called about a loan complication—they need your signature immediately. She replies that she wishes she could, but her husband is cleaning the barbeque, and their younger child is napping.

You've never asked her for a favor before. You weren't thinking this qualified.

The Giver

Every year around your birthday she drives from San Francisco—usually bearing a cinnamon torte she's baked because it's your favorite—then offers to watch your kids for the weekend so you can relax at a spa. In grad school she designed your bridesmaids' dresses, and after the divorce, called you every Monday for a year. Once, when you telephoned to ask about working a backstitch, she arrived the next day with her sewing machine in hand. She never misses your kids' performances—as elephants, giraffes, and grapes—and watches with a smile so tender you'd think those children were hers.

One Thanksgiving she calls to say hi, then promptly bursts out crying. Her credit cards are maxed and she can't pay her bills. She didn't want to tell you, but you're the most practical person she knows, so you get a sitter and drive up north to work out a plan, which you type in Excel. The weekend is spent circling classified ads, eating vinegar chips, and watching *Bridget Jones's Diary*. Your friend doesn't ask, but before you leave you write her a check, to get her started.

The following summer you lend her your car. The summer after, you pay her Urgent Care bill. The year after that you finally ask why she hasn't found a job. She says it's because her debts are so high that her wages will be garnished directly from her account—any pay she receives would be withdrawn from the bank so she wouldn't see a cent. Instead she closes all her accounts, volunteers at Hospice, and records audio books for the blind.

Still, you slip her cash every time you see her. After awhile you begin to slip her less, because it occurs to you that you might be enabling something unhealthy.

With some of the money you give her, she buys your kids birthday presents.

The Confidante
When her mood is up and the two of you are out binging on tapas and coconut mojitos, you hold your breath and ask about her recent biopsy results. She tells you everything came back clean so you share a caramel flan, then compare notes on Diflucan versus Monistat for yeast. She asks how you've been feeling since your ex's Disney wedding, and

when you tell her about the smile you forced when your son said his stepmother was pretty, she squeezes your hands between warm nubby fingers that glitter with moonstone and jade. As always you promise to get together more, though it's hard with work and with children.

When it's been too long since you've heard from her, you call but nobody answers. You suspect she's lying beside the phone, her copper hair sandwiched between mattress and pillow. You can't dig her out—she's told you as much—but you leave a voicemail anyway. You say things like, *just checking in* and *miss you*. You hope your concern will diminish her pain by an ounce or two that day.

At three o'clock you consider driving over to her house. You could toss her that beaded shawl she loves and drag her out for happy hour. But the fridge is empty, your daughter's inhaler is lost, and your son's toes have bored holes through fronts of his sneakers. Instead you stop at CVS, then Foot Locker, and Vons. While you wait for your son outside karate you text her, *Call me!*

When the chicken has been roasted, the dishes scrubbed and stacked, the garbage taken out, and the wet towels picked up off the floor, you remind your kids to brush their teeth—you'll be in to say goodnight. With the doors locked you rub your eyes and plug in your phone to charge. Her text reads: *Come over? Feeling blue.* The clock says 8:57.

Her house is a twenty-five minute drive. If you called right now the neighbor's daughter might come sit. Two Advil could take the edge off your headache, and the kids would be asleep anyway. But tomorrow's alarm is set for six, and it's your day to carpool. Then there's breakfast at eight, a new client at ten, and as usual, all the billing. You haven't been to the gym in weeks.

You drop to the couch and reread her text. It's now 8:59.

You rest your eyes and wonder what kind of friend you really are.

We Work in Miraculous Cages

by Brenda Peynado

I was one of millions of college graduates trying to pay off student loans and credit card debt on minimum wage. I worked in a hair salon as a receptionist from nine to five and at a veterinary emergency hospital on nights and weekends. I had a boyfriend, but he kept wanting to take my clothes off in the few hours I could sleep. At the vet hospital, I ran around yanking the cats out of their carriers by the scruff of the neck, weighing the dogs, calling for triage, sorting through mountains of paperwork. Sometimes you turned around and a dog hacked up an organ, or a cat came in on the Fourth of July with a firecracker through its head, or a police dog was being rushed in from a gang shooting, or a ferret had escaped its cage and vomited green all over the hospital.

I was so angry, at myself, at the clients. Angry at the salt of the earth, the farmers who brought in their pot-bellied pigs, the welfare poor's shaking hands as they handed over their animals. These were most of the people we saw at the emergency vet. People with money, with time, they shuttled their animals to their regular vets as soon as they sensed something amiss. Everyone else tried to wait it out, only brought us the animals when they were near death. I started telling the hysterical owners clutching their dying pets, It will be okay. But after a few months and enough dogs and cats dying a day, my own life like molecules that would not bind, like the electricity of a heart that fades and will not restart, I knew it would not be okay.

Then I started to say, We'll try everything we can.

But that was even worse, because everything we could try cost money that less and less people seemed to have, and we all had seen where trying had gotten us.

At the hair salon, I checked people in and out of their appointments, answered the phones, counted cash. I had to stand up behind the counter. The owner had thrown away the stools because he thought sitting made us look lazy, less ready to serve. I also doubled as an office manager because they couldn't afford to hire a second person. It was a high-end salon, so it's not that they couldn't. They wouldn't. I got a few extra dollars an hour, but it wasn't enough to make a dent, not when I was paying twice my rent in credit card and student loan repayments.

They would call me into the back to shampoo some-one's head or massage hands if they were in a pinch. These people I shampooed, they were sequins and glitz and glam, fake breasts, balloon lips pinned into smiles, the stretched faces of age artificially preserved, all those people who could afford to spend money just to wash their hair, or get their eyebrows arched in just the perfect way. I did not want to hear about their lives. I was content to watch the water swirling and their shampoo bubbling and guess at the viscosity of the liquid.

When the person was young, I didn't mind it. They thought they had their whole life ahead of them, and while I massaged their hands, I wished this for them. With the older women, it was different. I thought about how they had spent not just their lives, but our lives too, gobbled up or snorted up or injected into their face all that good fortune of the eighties and the dot-com boom etcetera, them laying their head back into the shampoo bowl and me wasting all my understanding about the world on mashing their skin over their bones.

At the vet hospital, a woman brought in a python in a cardboard box, bleeding heavily, chunks missing from his body.

Triage to the front, I breathed into the speakerphone.

How can I help you? I said.

A tech appeared and took the box away from her into the back.

It's a long story, she said. I feed it live rats, because that's better for them, you know? I send one wriggling down into the tank, and my python eats it. Well, this week it wasn't hungry, so I left the rat in there, thinking when he finally got up the hunger he'd pounce.

Oh no, I said, shoving the paperwork at her.

The rat started chewing on my python instead.

The rat ate the python? I repeated.

A sobbing girl ran into the hospital, yelling, Someone please tell me if my dog is alive.

Triage to the front, I breathed into the speakerphone, and triage came and stretchered the dog into the hospital. Alive, the tech mouthed as he headed to the back.

So I made this girl and her father who walked in afterwards fill out the paperwork. She was skinny, her eyebrows tweezed to slivers, and you could see every blue vein in her legs.

Then a man came in with a cat that hadn't peed in days, which meant its bladder would probably rupture. Then a couple walked in with a dog, a big one, seizing and twitching in their arms.

Triage to the front. Triage to the front. I wanted to sit, because my feet hurt, but then I needed to stand because my back hurt, and I wanted to sleep, and for a moment, I wanted to cut my brain from my body, like a sinking ship throwing baggage overboard. I was the python, eaten by a thing I was told I would master.

My boyfriend brought me dinner. He felt apologetic for an argument we'd had the night before. My boyfriend had found a real job at a bank, but we all knew his position was precarious. He was one of the lucky ones. When I mentioned this, he'd huff and argue. He would cover the rent for me for a few days, until the next paycheck came, but he was trying to pay off his student debt, too. It's not like he was hoarding it, he said. He believed he'd gotten everything entirely of his own merit. But there was not a one of us without merit, so said the certificates mailed to us by the merit-scholarship-this and the merit-scholarship-that we'd had thrown at us during college. He didn't even have the highest test scores; my best friend Gemma did.

Mostly we had argued about my laziness. I was never home, so I didn't cook, I didn't clean, and still I could barely pay rent and my bills. I was driving my car around uninsured.

The night before, I discovered he'd put one of my dirty dishes on my side of the bed. I'm not your maid, was what he said in defense. Clean up after yourself.

I had spent hours cleaning up after dogs that had puked on themselves, cats that had defecated all over their carriers, and undetermined ooze at the vet's office; plus bowls of chemical ammonia, stick and slime from hair products that crusted the walls at the hair salon. When I came home, I had six hours and counting until I had to be awake again. The very one thing I wanted not to do, I told him, was to clean up after myself, the one thing I had control over in this new life.

Look at me, he said. I have time to cook for myself and clean and run to keep myself in shape.

So I'm gaining weight, I said. You're the one with all the free time. Would it kill you to clean a dish?

It's never one dish, he said.

My life is on hold, I said.

He reminded me of my complicity in all that, how I'd spent thousands on credit cards, banking on promises that I would pay it off later with my new job and my education. He said, You put yourself in this position. When you live like a king in a time of debt, you invite the ransomer to come collecting.

What are you, Shakespeare? I yelled.

He liked to lunge suddenly towards an expensive lamp I'd bought using student loans, or the antique chair from craigslist, or the designer clothes that sat on my hangers, as if to tear, break, and smash.

I'm taking everything you own to Goodwill, he said. And that's the sad part; you wouldn't even notice they were gone.

Please don't, I begged.

The truth was I didn't remember the last time I had turned that lamp on, or sat in that antique chair. I was too busy wearing a uniform emblazoned with some company logo or another to wear my expensive clothes. Smile, said one uniform. The veterinarian's was embroidered with the EKG line of a perfect, healthy heartbeat. The hair salon's logo was a kite lifting a boy and a girl up into the air. Underneath the logo said, Reach for your perfect self.

He wasn't a bad guy, my boyfriend. I knew he wanted love as much as I did. But I had no time to give him the kind of love we were both convinced we needed. Picnics or long walks in the park, talking until late into the night. The night before, when I came home and saw the desperation on his face, I saw a tick mark adding one more to-do on the list I drowned in. When I smiled at him, it felt like chucking sand down an unfillable sinkhole. Then that's when I found the dish crusted with spaghetti sauce on my side of the bed. My situation was only temporary, we promised each other when we made up.

So he brought me dinner at the vet hospital the next day. He was apologetic. Often, he brought these elaborate meals with five courses that he had cooked, which I would have to shovel down in cold mouthfuls when my bosses' backs were turned. I wanted to thank him like he deserved. I could see hurt on his face when I barely had a second to say hi, grab the food, turn around again to the couple with the seizing dog and the black-smiled girl who was screaming at me.

After he left, I calmed down the couple with the seizing dog. I had to pee and I'd been holding it since my shift at the salon. I threw the remaining paperwork at one of the vet techs, Jose, and went to the bathroom. I called Gemma on the toilet, the only way I got to talk to her anymore. She was one of these blonde Hispanics who looked so American, you wouldn't even know she was born in another country. Smartest one out of all of us. She'd done everything that had ever been asked of her. We'd barely seen each other since graduation.

How are you? I asked, my bladder emptying with relief. From outside the bathroom, I could hear another person hysterical about their animal walk into the hospital. I locked the door.

If I tell you, Gemma said, I'm going to cry.

So we caught up quickly on other friends instead. We were all hitting our heads on ceilings erected after graduation overnight. The more we worked our minimum-wage jobs, the less likely we were to get a real job, the ones we coveted, with health insurance and salary and paid sick days and holidays when we could rest. But it wasn't factory work, like some of our grandparents; it wasn't coal mining, like so many of our ancestors thought their descendants would be doing for all of eternity. It was not macheteing sugar cane in Latin America like our parents had come here to avoid. We were not being hunted down by the government. So how could we complain? But we were the valedictorians, the straight-laced, the work-hard-to-reap-our-rewards sort of students, and our parents and teachers had told us we were special, we were stars, we were almost our perfect selves, and so we had expected so much more.

Afterwards, the ones with the seizing dog elected to euthanize it. That's how I'd been told to say it, election, as if everything we'd come to we had chosen. They were told that epilepsy would cost them thousands. Sure, the dog could have a close to normal life. He was already out of the seizure and kept trying to climb into their laps. But the couple had kids and a mortgage. So they decided to put him down. They were pretty calm about it. It was just like falling asleep, the woman kept repeating. Then, when they were checking out, the woman had one of those moments when you realize what you've done. She laid her head down on the counter. It was already too late. Their dog was dead.

I know you think I'm terrible, she sobbed. God forbid anyone would ever make that decision for me, to put me down because of money.

We do what we do, I said, which was not meant to be a consolation.

She straightened up, and her husband pulled her out the door.

The skinny girl and her father were another matter. They'd been told they could save the dog, which had been attacked by a bigger dog from a neighboring farm. But it, too, would cost thousands. IV bags, catheters, antibiotics, surgery with lasers to graft skin and sew together muscles.

Do it all, she said, but I don't have any money.

Credit cards, I had been trained to suggest.

I have none, she said, but do it all. Save my dog.

Or we can have you fill out an application for credit, I said. Or you can call friends and we can take their payment over the phone.

Then she was hysterical. You don't understand, she says. I can try all those but even if someone would lend me the money—which they won't—eventually I have to pay them back and. I. Have. No. Money.

Her father looked on silently. There wasn't anything to do. She didn't have any money and I didn't have any money and we didn't have any money, and the dog was going to die and I hated the both of us for it. She was crying over the dog that she couldn't save, her blue veins showing through her skin like the state of the world melting into rivers, and then she was laughing at herself because what else could she do? The dog died.

A few weeks later, a girl came into the hair salon with hair she described as thinning. She told me while I squeezed shampoo onto her head that she was feeling rundown. Her husband had lost his job and she was working overtime to make up the difference. She was barely older than me, maybe late twenties. She said she passed the salon every day on her way to work and finally decided to treat herself.

As I shampooed her, her hair fell out from her head in giant clumps and tangled around my fingers. I was preoccupied in horror and fascination as the hairs slithered down the drain, when she asked me if I'd gone to school to be a hair stylist.

Oh no, I said, I'm not a hair stylist, I'm an engineer, I'm just doing this in-between.

Hair stylists at the other shampoo bowls glared at me and my snobbery.

I will not be here forever! I wanted to yell in defiance. Meanwhile I lifted my hands up from the bowl with a web of this girl's hair netting between my fingers.

The other stylists shook their heads side-to-side in threatening ways.

Sell her the thinning scalp shampoo, one mouthed.

Another one pointed to the lavender-scented oils we were trained to push on the clients.

But I couldn't help myself. You should be going to a doctor, I said, and not the hair salon.

The next day, I got called into the salon on my day off, for yet another meeting I wasn't getting paid for. I thought I was going to lose that job.

We think you have an attitude problem, said the owner.

I couldn't deny it.

Stop telling people that you do other things during the day, they said. This is now your real job. They're paying for some degree of servitude. It makes them uncomfortable to imagine their college professor massaging their scalp.

Must my mind be a slave? I asked.

Your mind has nothing to do with it. You are who we tell you to be.

In bed that night, my boyfriend said, You've always been tough. You can wait this out. We'll get through this.

He was massaging my back. I closed my eyes.

What if there's no end to this darkness, I said.

He switched off the light, rolling his hand over my stomach. Next thing I knew, I was asleep. The earth turned under my feet like a tornado. The sky, in between my job in the mornings and my job at night, was a gray blur announcing the physics of pressure and fluid dynamics, atoms and molecules whirling and collecting in giant piles.

On my one day off a week, I slept. If I had an interview, I'd give up my day off and don a suit and try my best to convince someone to give me a salary. I had a degree in Astronautics and I could tell you how in your very own body the molecules methylated, I could build a motor that would take you to Jupiter, I could tell you what love was in the most abstract of terms, and none of that meant anything to anyone. The year I graduated was when the space shuttle program was dismantled. Not that it mattered. Even most of my friends in fields that hadn't died were searching for jobs.

I ironed a collared shirt and the suit I had bought on loans when I should have been sleeping, when I should have been cleaning or keeping house or eating. My boyfriend had given up trying to lure me into our bed, and he lay there, snoring under a moon chugging forward, a locomotive swimming circles around the earth to eternity.

I was called to interview with a stereo company, for a job involving engineering speakers and sound waves. I interviewed twice with an oil company, once as a project manager, once as an engineer. With a technology audit firm, with a cell phone company in R&D, with another company that it turns out wasn't really hiring. They just wanted to feel out the job pool, apparently. In the cell phone company's interview, a panel of three men and one woman in their fifties interrogated me from behind clipboards.

When they asked me about my greatest weakness, I said I worked too hard and overextended myself.

Design an evacuation plan for San Francisco, an interviewer said. Go.

How many traffic lights are there in all of Manhattan? Go.

How many quarters would it take to reach the moon?

Okay, I said. I estimated the quarters, the distance to the moon divided by the width of quarters factoring in the latitude position on earth and the time of the month and the time of day for deviation. Figuring all that, I said, you would need 1,042,707,234 quarters to reach the moon.

They nodded. One of them closed her eyes. Another put his feet on the conference table.

However, I continued, that would be about 25 billion dollars. It might take fewer quarters if you used them to buy a space shuttle from the now-defunct space shuttle program, plus staff and research, and used that to reach the moon.

They grunted in approval. An awkward silence slithered between us. The interview ended. They all shook my hand.

We're really excited about you, they said. You seem like exactly what we're looking for. We'll be making our decision very, very soon.

How'd it go? my boyfriend asked.

I always think they go well.

You'll get through this, he said, and I noticed he didn't say we.

A few of the interviewers were nice enough to put me out of my misery and tell me that another qualified candidate was selected for the job. Most of them never called, despite polite emails asking when they would come to their decisions. They would all but throw the job into my lap, the interview bloated with promises. I'd be in hoping agony for weeks. Then one day I would wake up realizing they weren't going to call. I would trudge into the hair salon or the veterinarian and know I would never be anything except a receptionist. I felt like a gerbil in an exercise wheel trying to climb that ladder of quarters to reach the moon, and the wheel goes and goes and goes without the moon getting any bigger.

Months passed, and I couldn't even tell you what I had done except work. I marked the time in terms of friends that had moved away, looking for jobs in the bigger cities where everyone was crowding. Every weekday I drove from the hair salon to the veterinarian's across town. The only way I ever saw anyone, if they didn't walk into my work, was driving past them. I saw some old friends and we honked and waved, and then sped off again because we were late and every second counted. I had to be careful because once I'd been pulled over for speeding and being uninsured. Please, I told the cop, I can't afford the ticket. He was one of those cops with a smirk. The law is the law, he said. I put that ticket on a credit card. I sped even faster from work to work to clock in earlier so I could pay off the credit card.

One night, I got home and my boyfriend was already asleep. I showered, put on a silk shirt and soft leggings, the clothes I could no longer wear during the day and I had paid so dearly for. My feet throbbed. I slipped between the covers smelling like lavender, and for just a moment I was not ready to sob.

He stirred. His hand reached for my stomach and he said, Mmm, because it was covered in silk.

Not tonight, I said.

His eyes opened. When? he said.

On my day off, I said.

We need to talk, he said.

Now we were both awake and listening to the cars outside, rushing like spaceships towards the moon.

Please, I said, Can it wait until tomorrow? I have a job interview on my lunch break. I have to sleep.

What if you never get the job? How can we live like this?

So we're going to do this now? I said.

I keep waiting, he said. I keep waiting for the person you used to be, who was wonderful, who was loving. He tugged on my shirt, the silk crushed in his soft hands.

I am that person, I said. This is not me.

He said, There is no such thing as who you are. Only what you do. Over and over. Like bringing you dinner at the vet. Love is a verb.

I love you, I said.

Prove it, he said. He kept tugging at the hem.

I appreciate everything you do for me, I said, too tired to cry.

He yanked, and all the buttons flew up into the air. For a moment I thought they would stay up there, buttons frozen and floating above us. They looked like coins, spinning and glittering in moonlight. But then they came back down and skittered against the floor.

I got out of the bed. I got down on hands and knees to collect all the buttons scattered around the room. I said, Could you even tell me how many millions of these buttons it would take to reach the sun?

Why are we together? he said. What are we doing except subsisting and waiting?

I held my hands out, palms open. I had nothing to offer. I wanted to fight, I wanted to love, I wanted to sleep. I remembered going on a picnic on the university greens, studying together, designing for my thesis a space shuttle capsule to his measurements, both of us standing on the dorm roof ready take the landscape underneath us by storm.

He must have felt guilty. He got out of bed and tried to hold me with my shirt flapping open.

I pushed him away. I said, I have to sleep. I can interview to be your girlfriend soon, but not tonight.

I've been meaning to tell you, he said, grabbing at his head with his hands. I'm no longer hiring for the position.

I bet, I said. I poured the buttons into a drawer and collapsed into bed. I closed my eyes.

He began to pack his bags.

I couldn't afford the apartment, and he knew it. Behind my eyelids, I called triage to the front. I climbed quarters to the moon. Somewhere in the craters, if I kept searching, I'd find a man at rest.

The next day, I crammed what I could in my trunk, and a sleeping bag in the backseat. I left a note telling my now ex-boyfriend he could take everything to Goodwill. I drove to the salon wound so tightly with expectation that had I been flicked with a finger, I would have snapped.

Gemma walked into the salon. She slapped a ten on the counter. I had to borrow the money, she said, so give me what you can.

I'm so glad you're here, I said, but why are you here?

I heard you broke up, she said.

I can't talk about it, or I won't be able to get through to-day.

I brought her to the back to give her a hand massage, intending to pocket the cash and give it back to her. I rubbed her palms with my thumbs. For the first time in so long, I wasn't angry about where I was or what I was doing.

I have something to tell you, she announced. I'm moving back to Venezuela.

My god, I said. You don't even remember that country. You can't even speak proper Spanish anymore.

My mom says I have a great-aunt who will take me in.

Stay, I said. I'll play hooky, and we'll have lunch.

She laughed softly. I hear there are jobs there, she said.

I knew it was a lie. These bodies were our cages. I wished so hard to be just the cage, this miraculous cage of atoms, with nothing but the wind inside. I wanted Flowers for Algernon but in reverse: the part of me that expected so much more dying and withering into a seed, blooming again into someone who lived the life of work like in it there was sustenance.

You're shaking, she said. Tell me what happened.

I rubbed lotion over Gemma's palms slowly. I closed my eyes. I could feel myself emptying. Then I felt her heartbeat with one hand on her wrist, more than just iron and oxygen and cells. I held her hand. A feeling flooded me I'd forgotten how to name.

That night at the vet, a cat's bladder exploded, a lizard lost its eye, one of the interviewers emailed to say they'd hired another candidate for the position. I called triage to the front, and I tried not to think about the future, sleeping that night in my car. I muzzled the dogs that curled their lips around their teeth with fear in their eyes. It's like they could smell how expendable they were, despite all the love in the world, despite how many times they sat and fetched and played dead and spun around in a circle. One dog kept standing up then sitting, over and over, and the owner kept saying, That's a good girl. Good girl. Good girl.

A tech called me to the back operating room. The vet and three techs huddled over a Dalmatian with her stomach flapped open. They pulled little wriggling gelatinous balls from the hole—an emergency C-section.

Grab a puppy, yelled the vet. There are too many puppies and not enough techs.

She handed me one of these hot, gelatinous blobs. Inside the brown mess was a furry creature with its eyes closed. I followed the techs' lead, using the suction wand to grab the placenta from its eyes and nose and mouth.

Wake it up, the vet told me. Beat it up. It's what the mother does, swings it around in her teeth and bats it with her paws until it starts crying, except this mother is knocked out from the anesthetic.

So we flung our puppies up and down, we rolled them out like fingers of dough on the operating table, we danced with them. The doctor brought out another brown ball from the stomach, set it down on the table. The doctor said, Leave it. There aren't enough of us.

But I thought it wasn't fair that something came into this world in which there just wasn't enough. So I sucked the placenta from the puppy's face as best I could with one hand, while shaking the first puppy with the other. I rolled both next to each other on the table, hoping to keep the second puppy warm and that any shaking of the first would reverberate into the second. Behind me, the doctor announced she'd lost the mother's heartbeat and she was starting defibrillation.

We kept with the puppies. My body, this miraculous cage, its electric atoms, danced. I waltzed with them towards the moon. I shook them. I wanted them to wail for milk they would never get. I beat them up until they cried.

"We Work in Miraculous Cages" originally appeared in *Quarterly West*.

The Tick and the Tocking

by Chelsea Sutton

1.

Uncle Poke dies face down in his beef stew.

There are eight of us at the dinner table when this happens. Well, seven if you don't count Uncle Poke, who, by definition, is no longer anywhere in particular. Seven bodies with spoons raised or mouths frozen in mid-chew, and one body slumped over, with bits of beef stew splash back stuck to its bald head.

Which is funny. Because Uncle Poke had a full, though thinning, head of hair moments before he died.

2.

I was wrong to mention moments. There may have been seconds or days or months or decades between Uncle Poke's hair and his death.

I shouldn't speak in terms of Time.

3.

Our plates and bowls are suddenly empty. No one can continue to eat, even if they wanted to.

There is much discussion of the body. My Aunt Miranda lets out a delayed scream of despair. My cousins Bill and Jules, twin boys with freckled faces, hold their mother's arms as she prepares to faint.

My own mother, having been pursing her lips in thought since Poke keeled over, towers darkly over the body and feels for a pulse. It looks to me like she's feeling for it in the wrong place on his neck, but I don't correct her. It doesn't seem to matter.

Aunt Miranda never faints.

4.

Through this activity, I've been mostly watching my father. He is leaning on his elbows, face in his hands. As I watch him I see wrinkles carve themselves in his skin. He loses ten pounds. His hair turns gray and thins around the back. When he lifts his face, he has bags under his eyes and his cheeks are drooping.

My heart crawls into my throat and strangles my vocal cords. I make a pathetic chirping sound.

5.

On my way to the bathroom, my little sister Sophie grabs my arm.

"I think I'm taller. My legs hurt. I feel taller. Do I look taller to you?"

She is. And so are the twins.

She will need to change clothes to make room for her height and freshly grown breasts. The twins will have stubble on their chins.

6.

In the bathroom, I avoid the mirror.

I breathe. It takes me a while to remember how to cry. A while. No. That's probably not right. It could take no while at all. But I remember. And I do. For a while. Or not.

7.

A period of Time goes by, but I cannot tell how long it is. I should not try to even guess.

A crackling and fizzling sound comes out of the radio. Then, a deep voiced announcer says:

"Attention. Time is officially moving forward. Repeat. Time is officially moving forward. Please take the usual precautions."

Aunt Miranda tries to faint again. She is unsuccessful.

8.

The sun sets.

I spend the night wandering the house. I listen to my parents breathing. I watch Sophie mumbling in her sleep in a bed too small for her.

For once, I wish Time would stop at night, when every-one else is asleep, when I wander, alone, watching over them, keeping them safe and tucked away.

I stare out my bedroom window at the empty sidewalk. I remember a face.

The sun rises again. This is Time progressing. Or so I'm told.

9.

Across town, the elementary school is flooded with teenagers in ill-fitting clothes. Newly minted adults are roaming the halls of the high schools. It takes a great amount of Time to sort out who belongs where.

This is a usual problem. The problem of where one belongs.

10.

Several women go into labor, only to have the baby grow into a walking-talking child in a matter of minutes. They never even have Time to hold the baby in their arms.

Some women who didn't know they were pregnant suddenly grow large bellies and give birth in their kitchens, in the backs of cars, at the grocery store, at the office, while making love to their husbands. The babies grow quickly and move into the guest rooms. Some of these women have miscarriages. Like terrible, painful, swift stomach aches requiring a great deal of cleaning up afterwards.

In a matter of minutes. Minutes. I don't feel I'm using the word correctly.

11.

There are many like Uncle Poke who die from heart attacks, sudden onsets of cancer, or old age. They die at their dinner tables, in their beds, at work. Some fall off ladders, are hit with poorly aimed bowling balls at the local alley, slip and hit their head by the swimming pool—so their death is doubly assured.

A few accidents are had by young people—brand new teenagers not quite used to that strange way their chemicals are balanced, the way their bodies move. Some are in the road when someone dies while driving a car.

In some places, the youth that die are called tragedies. Here, it all looks the same. At least to me.

12.

All these things happen as I leave my parents' house. My mother, her wrinkles, her gray, her thin arms, begs me to stay.

"We don't know how long this Tocking will last," she says. "You need to stay close by. The family needs to be together." Her lightly withered hand is holding on to mine.

"I won't go far," I say. And it is not a lie.

13.

The Tocking. That's what they like to call this period—when Time catches up with itself. There's the Tick and then the Tocking. Time stands still. And then it runs like hell.

Everyone hopes to be stuck in some lovely moment during the Tick. You never know how long you'll be stuck there, after all. And you never know what will happen once it's over.

Uncle Poke's death, as an example. Where will Aunt Miranda go? Bill and Jules were now grown men with libidos and hungers. Last time, we were able to get the whole family together. Eating a meal we could all agree on. That wouldn't happen again.

I am not planning to return home.

14.

There are always a few who race to the outskirts of town, once Time starts up again. They think if they run far enough and fast enough that they will escape it. That Time will move forward at a steady pace, that there will be no stopping or starting or speeding up or slowing down. Just a steady march of Time. But they are fooling themselves. There is no such place.

Some give up and head back. Others get stuck out there. Running and running and running and going nowhere for who knows how long.

When the Tocking happens, most end up dying from a burst heart.

15.

I walk to my single apartment near the center of town. There is a funeral procession marching in the middle of the road toward the cemetery. At least fifteen coffins in hearses, truck beds, horse drawn carts, or being carried by pallbearers. There is no Time for single funerals anymore. No Time. There will be another procession later in the day that will carry Uncle Poke's body. I won't be there.

I whisper a goodbye under my breath.

16.

A few teenagers push past me on the sidewalk as I search for my keys. The teenagers have it the best right about now. They have new bodies, new minds, new desires and strengths, more than they know what to do with.

During the Tocking, they are always running circles in the streets, eating stacks of hamburgers at the diners and fast food joints, playing music loud and thumping, writing terrible poetry, getting into fights.

Many make love in the backs of cars or quietly in their rooms while their parents are out.

17.

I was a teenager during a Tocking. I fell in love with a boy named Charlie. With green eyes and brown silky hair.

We made clumsy, sloppy love in my bedroom. The bedroom at my parents' house. The bedroom that has not changed, except for a new layer of dust. There is always a layer of dust that settles on things during a Ticking.

We lay awake all night, whispering, laughing, arms around each other, never parting until it was necessary. We made a list of moments we'd like to be stuck in, moments for the Ticking. We came up with twenty-five.

From my bedroom window, I watched him hurry away from my house as the end was coming close. He stopped at the end of the sidewalk, looked up at me, whistled a good-bye. As I watched, I almost felt Time stop, like the Ticking had come early this time. But I think it was just for me.

Occasionally Time will do that. It will stop just for you.

18.

I can't find my keys, so I think about breaking in. I had hoped to spend the next However Long reading in the dim light of my one-room apartment, reading the same few beautiful sentences over and over and drinking a cup of hot coffee, coffee that would never be cold and never be finished. Until it suddenly was.

We came up with a list of twenty-five. This is the only one I can remember.

I don't know how to break into a fourth story apartment. So I head toward the town square. Toward the library.

19.

In the square, there is the usual scene. Protesters outside the government building, rallying for banishment of the Time-tables, a return to steady rhythms. No more waiting and panic, waiting and panic.

The crowd waves sloppy hand painted signs, signs painted in haste several Tockings ago, they chant and strum guitars and march and dance. Some have been at this rally since forever. Whatever forever means.

I see my sister Sophie near the back of the crowd leaning against a wall with a young man. She has a woman's curves, a woman's face, a woman's smile. I barely recognize her. She doesn't see me.

20.

The library is closed. No one bothered to open it up this Tocking. Or perhaps the librarian died inside, and someone will be in for a big mess the next time around.

There are several cases of new books sitting on the steps. A delivery. There is always a delivery of new books to the stores and libraries. Always a run of new television show episodes and a string of newspapers.

Books and scripts written in years that had been churning in the minds of writers for seconds.

Wait. Years. Seconds. Reverse that.

I flip through a few titles. I find random pages and read words until I find a string of them I like. That's the book I take. It's hard covered, heavy and weathered looking even though it is brand new.

21.

A vote is being taken in the square. It's always the same vote. A vote for something the government has no control over anyway.

I hear my sister scream, even over the din of the protesters, the yells of voting. The young man she was with has her pinned to the wall and she's pushing hard against him.

I rush to her side and pull him off of her. I slam the book in my hand across his face. He bleeds and whimpers and runs away. He'll now spend the next However Long with a bleeding and broken nose.

Sophia looks at me. She squints. She doesn't recognize me at first. I realize I haven't looked in the mirror yet. I have no idea what I look like now. How old I am. If she's, what, sixteen or eighteen, then I must be at least thirty. Can't be so bad.

She hugs me, kisses me on the cheek, whispers in my ear. "See you at home." And she runs off.

I love her. Especially in this moment. But I'll never have enough Time to know her. Time enough.

22.

There is a spatter of the boy's blood on the cover of the book. I am sure, without a doubt, that I will enjoy reading it now, no matter how long that will be.

23.

I do not want to wake into the next Tocking to watch my parents keel over like Uncle Poke. I am embarrassed to be leaving that burden on Sophie. But I like goodbyes to be on my own terms. I want to want something else besides the next moment. Moment.

I always feel I'm using that word wrong.

24.

A few painters and repairmen are working on the storefronts and government buildings. Making them clean and sleek again. Even the buildings show their age once Time moves forward.

These men use their Time out of the Tick to beautify. They take their jobs seriously. Most get stuck up there on those ladders, hammering one last nail, painting one last stroke.

These are the men who die from the fall.

25.

I settle in a pub further off the square, the only place as dim and depressing as my one room apartment.

I find a place at the bar, order a Jack and ginger, and settle in for a good drunken read for However Long.

When someone whistles behind me.

It's Charlie. Older, but the same green eyes that stared up at me from the sidewalk However Long ago.

"It's good to see you," he says. "It's been … you know."

"I know," I say.

"May I join you?" he says. He sits on the stool next to me without waiting for an answer.

"I don't think this Tocking will last much longer. Don't you have a better moment to hurry off to?" I smooth my hands over the cover of the book, over the dried blood from the teenage boy with the perpetual broken nose.

"Not this time," says Charlie. He toasts the book in front of me with his whiskey sour. "Which one was this? Twenty-five?"

"I don't remember exactly," I say. I feel my face flush.

"Then I suppose we have a lot of catching up to do," Charlie says.

I feel it happening. Time is slowing down. But when I look at the others in the bar, they move normally, they don't seem stuck at all. It's for me. The slowing down.

I enjoy it for as long as it lasts. And then I answer.

"And I guess we have all the Time in the world to do that. To catch up or read or talk or drink or ... what else was on our list?"

Charlie leans in and kisses me. We kiss. For several moments.

Moment. That's right this time.

"What would you rather do first?" I open the book to the page with the beautiful sentences. And I take a sip from my glass.

And I feel it happening. Time slowing. Again. But I don't know if it is real or only mine. And it doesn't much matter.

"The Tick and the Tocking" originally appeared in *Bourbon Penn*.

A Meditation on Dresses
by Marcia Walker

Dress #1

The first dress you remember is creamy white, covered with wild flowers the size of nickels. The blooms are condiment-coloured: mustard, ketchup, marmalade, and the foliage a neon relish. You wear it everywhere. It smells like you, a mixture of calamine lotion, baby shampoo, peanut butter, and grass. The curved collar folds over your clavicle and a bow cinches your five-year-old waist. Your mother helps you with the long zipper up the back in the morning. Her fingers, cold as logic, brush your skin, making the bones of your back stick out.

—Hold still. Stop wriggling.

Her touch is utilitarian; she doesn't like to linger. She stiffens if you hug her too long. The dress is what touches your body. You're aware every time it grazes your kneecaps, how the worn cotton sleeves brush your elbows and wrists. During nap you suck on the fraying cuffs.

In kindergarten your class sings "Where have all the flowers gone?" Years later you will find it odd, a meditation on death sung by five-year-olds, but now you like how the melody and words fit together. "Long tiiiime paaaasssinnng." You sing the loudest except at the refrain because you stop then and wait for them to point at your dress. All those pudgy four and five-year-old fingers, dirt squashed under the nails, aimed at you, as if to say "that's where the flowers are. Look. Just look at them." You are where the flowers are.

Wear the dress until the grass has stained the elbows and the hem is up to your thighs. Your underwear shows when you sit cross-legged. You're wearing that dress when you tackle Jonathan P. at the Fun Fair and kiss him under the watermelon stand. Afterwards you twirl around, the hot pavement burning your feet, and the dress flies out. Cool air blows through your panties.

Dress #2

It's the year you wear black tights and oversized t-shirts every day and would like to forget you have a body. The dress is a fashion departure. A seamstress makes it because prom is special, once in a lifetime. Plus it's cheaper than The Bay. You go with your mom to Fabricland to choose the material. She holds reams of fabric next to your cheek, your head held in profile like a mug shot. Peacock blue. Royal blue. Ultramarine.

—Your skin is blotchy, your mom says. She doesn't like to say words like acne or zits.

You don't say anything but your silence is a protest. You chose a bluish purple, almost silk material, with a sheen.

—Don't go near any fires, it looks flammable.

—Oh come on, she says later —I was kidding. Don't be so sensitive.

Spaghetti straps make your arms appear thinner. Two frills below your waist camouflage your hips. Your mom suggests these styles and the seamstress agrees. When you try it on you look like someone older, someone with a sex life. Despite yourself, your views on fashion, your feminist ideals, you love the dress. You buy heels and shave your armpits. You wonder who you are as wet mats of black hair clog the shower drain.

The form-fitting style means you can't really dance or walk. This is a standing dress. There are photos of you in the dress standing on your lawn, your neighbour's lawn, in front of the green electrical box and next to Mike's rusted brown Chevrolet. Your mother insists on more photos. Her frenetic enthusiasm makes you wonder if she's jealous.

Go to prom. In the gym you gulp rum and Coke from a green thermos. Swallow, keep it down. Mike dances around you, jumping and flailing his arms to the ceiling. If only this was attractive. You bob to the music, keeping your legs together, worried the dress will tear at the seams. Your feet ache and so you ditch the pumps; their purple-blue dye staining your feet so they looked damaged and bruised. Mike stops dancing and watches you leave the dance floor. You are not a good prom date.

You peel off your control-top pantyhose in the bathroom and use toilet paper to wipe the deodorant that has piled in thick white rows under your arms. You stay too long in the stall, hiding, the cold sweat from the toilet bowl pooling against your calf, eventually running down to your ankle. Girls come and go, laughing. You think: I am, on a very deep level, a faker.

When the washroom is empty, you open the stall, stumble towards the mirror, and gaze into your eyes like a lover. Guns N' Roses' "Sweet Child O' Mine" plays, muffled from the gym. You whisper, I love you. You blow yourself a kiss. You do it again. Now mean it. Now kiss the mirror. Stacey Wheedon runs in, sees you, and then pukes before she reaches the stall.

Dress #3
—A good basic, the saleswoman says, eyeing you in the mirror. —Every woman should own a navy blue sheath. Just add some pearls and you can wear it for evening. So versatile.

You try not to feel intimidated by her, smoothing the dress over your hips and posing in front of the mirror, as jazz piano tinkles through unseen speakers. The silk lining is cool and weightless next to your skin. Very professional. The hem cuts sharp at the knees and the sleeves stop at your triceps. In the mirror your arms and legs look vaguely detachable and you wonder what it would feel like to have a stump for a body. At certain angles you can see your hip-bones jutting. This makes you confident, in control. You want him to see you in this dress.

—I'll take it.

Your fingers leave pin-drops of sweat on your credit card and you wipe them off on your shirt before handing the card to the saleswoman. Over two hundred dollars on an item of clothing. A first. You buy fake pearls as well and think: someday I'll go to cocktail parties.

It's your power dress. You save it for important days when you're the junior attached to his file, following him to court or a tribunal. On research days, when you're alone in your office, you wear your cheaper black suit with the loose hem. You're more articulate when you wear the sheath. Words like anathema and etymological slip into your conversations effortlessly. He says you have a good analytical mind one night when you're working late, but his eyes linger on your neck.

You work harder—an upcoming trial, a demanding client, it doesn't matter. Your hands smell of printer ink. There's a photo on his desk of him and his wife rollerblading, those tacky white helmets, and after the third week of working late you point to it and tell him his wife is pretty. Mmmmn, he says. You stay later than needed. You buy a matching navy blue blazer on the weekend to cover the sweat stains forming on the sheath. Half-moon salt stains under your arms.

In the morning you rush to put on the dress. It has a side zipper, hidden, seamless. Careful—twice you've zipped up your flesh. You nick yourself again. Small dots of blood form scabs like ladders up your ribs. Later, he kisses your skin, still sore, along the trail of the zipper.

—Take more time, he says, outlining your ribs with his index finger. Then he adds —This doesn't mean anything.

Wonder what he's referring to: The kiss? The cut from the zipper? The relationship? Don't ask for clarification.

Forget the daywear/nightwear separation—throw caution to the wind!—and wear the pearls with the dress to work. He asks you if you're going to a cocktail party. You tell him you're going on a date. Wait for signs of jealousy. He says that's good, you should get out more.

Consider forms of revenge: spitting in his coffee, lighting his office chair on fire, calling his wife. Decide to work harder. Question your self worth.

When you meet your mom for lunch (it doesn't happen often, the drive to the city wears her out), she says you look tired and thin. Then she complains about her fat stomach, fat thighs, fat knees, fat neck. She asks where you got the pearls. Roll a hard white ball between your thumb and forefinger and consider making up a boyfriend who gave them to you as a present. Let her question linger. Ask for the cheque.

—I used to have pearls like that, she says.

—Did you?

—You're just like me. I could never afford the real ones either.

Make a point of paying even though she holds her cash in front of you like sticky candy. She puts away her folded money and tentatively fondles the seam of your dress, her eyes soft, and murmurs —Expensive…

Show her the office. She always demands a tour. Don't linger. Avoid his office, his entire hallway. Don't introduce her to the partners. Don't introduce her to anyone except the support staff. Tell yourself you're doing this for her, saving her from embarrassment. She never went to university. She doesn't know anything.

—So this is where it all happens, she says.

Pity her. Then press the elevator button. Keep pressing until it arrives.

Dress #4

You meet in the produce department on a Saturday morning. You're wearing your "getting shit done" dress, $7.99, on sale at Winners. One hundred percent cotton jersey and shapeless, a pillowcase with two holes cut out for your arms. Changing into this dress is the first thing you do when you get home from work. You used to add a belt, but since you switched jobs you let it all hang out. The jersey reveals every imperfection of your body: the dimples on your thighs, the extra flaps of drooping skin tugging around your bra, the lines of your underwear. This used to bother you. Now you think: hell, at least I'm wearing underwear.

On the walk over to the grocery store you compared the dress to the colour of the sidewalk. If you laid down, you'd blend right in. Notice the polished concrete floor in the produce aisle of the grocery store and wonder if you'd blend in here. Resist lying down.

—Are these ripe? a short man asks, startling you and pointing to the stack of melons.

You think: what a lame come on. Really? Melons? Then you notice an oil stain next to your crotch and shimmy behind the grapes to hide it. He apologizes and says he really has no clue about these things. You shake the melon next to your ear, listening for its seeds sloshing and pass it back to him.

You say —Yes, these are ripe melons. You don't smile, not wanting to encourage him, but he's encouraged all the same.

Over the next few weeks it becomes clear you both grocery shop on Saturday mornings and a game develops. "What's ripe now?" He covers the gamut of fruit: watermelons, cantaloupes, pineapples, nectarines, plums, grapes. It's summer. There is a lot of fruit.

Somewhere between peaches and tomatoes you learn his name is Jeff, go for coffee, then out for a movie. You throw out the cement dress, embarrassed that you wore it in public, but also relieved that's how you met. He likes you in your most depressed state, which is a good sign he will stay with you through anything.

On Labour Day, when everyone else has left the city, you end up back at his place and make out standing in his hallway. His hands hold your shoulder blades like a steering wheel.

You say: Let's go inside.

His nervousness relaxes you. After a lot of jangling with his keys, he opens the door. His apartment is cleaner than yours with slick, shiny surfaces. "Look Ma, I can see myself," you want to say when you stare at your reflection in the TV stand. Don't say this. Mentioning your mother isn't sexy. Still, you hear her voice in your head saying: don't settle. Ignore the voice.

Dress #5
You get married. You wear a white dress.

Dress #6
It's the only dress that still fits this far into your second pregnancy. This baffles you because it's not a maternity dress and you found it used at a rummage sale. It still smells

of the previous owner (incense and pickling juice) and though you've saturated it in lavender oil, the old scent always wins out. You carefully sewed two ribbons so the back ties up and stretches the material tight over your belly. Arch your back, show it off.

The dress is inky black with tiny orange paisley patterns running through it. Henry, your four-year-old, says you should wear it for Halloween. You tell him you wore it when he was in your belly and he rubs your bump like it's a genie bottle, closing his eyes. When no magic happens, he loses interest.

Your mother arrives for dinner and you help her with her coat, purse, hat, and dollar store bags. She has not been to your house in almost a year and her clutter in the empty hallway seems out of place. Each plastic bag is filled with cheap toys, candy, and polyester baby clothes that you will throw out once she has left. Henry hides behind your leg. She takes out a bag of sour candies and tells him to catch. The candy lands at his feet. Jeff takes the bag from Henry and throws you a look when Henry starts to cry. He carries him wailing out of the room.

—If they're not crying about this, they're crying about that, your mother says and sighs, collapsing onto the couch.

—We don't give him treats, you say.

—Have I already done something wrong?

You make a tea and sit with her at the other end of the couch. Rub your belly to the rhythm of the clock, feeling an entire universe pulsing inside you. Black piles have formed along the tummy of the dress where your hands, Jeff's hands, your girlfriends' hands, co-worker's hands, and the trembling outreached hands of strangers have touched.

Your mother watches you. Her fingers rattle on the table. On an impulse you shimmy closer to her on the couch, take her hand in yours, and plunk it on your stomach. Wait for her to pull away. Her hand is as still as water. The unexpected heat of her palm seeps through the material. You think: we've changed. I've changed. We're better now.

She pulls away as the baby kicks your left rib.

—Did you feel that? you ask.

She straightens up and pats the pillow with two strong punches.

—I should probably eat soon. I don't want to get caught in traffic.

Several hours after she has left, you lie in bed with Jeff trying to get comfortable. He passes you an additional pillow for between your legs but doesn't say anything, still put out by your mother's visit. After a long moment in silence he says he doesn't want your mother coming over for Thanksgiving.

—You understand, right? She brings all that crap. And she never does anything with her grandson, she just lies on the couch the whole time. I don't get how the two of you lived together for so many years. You're nothing like her.

This is a compliment; it's kindly meant. Stop short of saying thank you.

An image of your mom springs into your mind. Her reflection in the store window, wearing her puffy grey Michelin Man coat. Your old Boxing Day tradition of window-shopping in the most expensive area of town. She stood stoically in the cold wind because she refused to step inside the fancy stores, too embarrassed in front of the sales staff. You both looked past your reflection to the floor-length purple dress, embroidered with silver beads.

—Imagine that, your mother said, her voice high and clear. —Like wearing moonlight.

Jeff is still talking and your focus returns to what he's saying.

—We'll just go to my parents' place at Thanksgiving, you'd probably prefer that anyway, right? It's not like we spend much time with her anyway.

You say it's no problem but something inside falls away. You decide it's not important. It's disposable. Like your appendix you can get by without it.

Dress #7

Find yourself staring into your closet more, blankly shifting the clothing, scraping the hangers to the side, clearing space, and searching for something that does not exist. You do not own this dress though you've carried it with you through the years. You imagine yourself wearing it. Your other self. The self you didn't become. Her.

The dress changes. Sometimes it's a thin yellow silk number, the colour of egg yolks. Another time it's a burgundy leather wrap dress. Sometimes you glimpse the dress before you go to bed, as your put down your book club book, on loan from the library. When you close your eyes it appears, a wedding dress, so enormous it needs its own storeroom. The ruffles poof out the door. Its extravagance makes you blush in the dark. Lately the dress sneaks up on you.

Talking to your oldest friend, Nancy, also recently divorced, while watching the Oscars pre-show fashion, the phone crooked between your shoulder and your ear, you tell her to check out the one in the crazy short number.

—The one nominated for best supporting?

—Oh my god, look at her. If she bent over we could see her ass. What was she thinking?

—Her legs are really skinny.

—Even if your legs are that skinny. Still.

—Hey, Nancy says, her voice changing, lower, with intent. You know what she's going to ask. —How's your mother?

—The same. She should be out by next week.

—Back home?

—No. I'm arranging a care facility.

—In the city?

—Closer to where she lives, I didn't think of here.

—Well, that's probably better in the long run. She sips her wine and sighs. —God I'd kill to have legs like that. Do you think she'll win best supporting?

Nancy takes a bathroom break at the commercials and you turn off the volume and rest the phone on your lap. The kids are with Jeff. The house is quiet. Closing your eyes you imagine the other life, the one that you could have had if you'd made bigger choices. The not good wife, the not good mother, the not good daughter. Picture yourself as her wearing a black drape, fine as warm breath. Material you would be afraid to touch, pages from an ancient book that disintegrate between your fingers, but she moves about comfortably, seductive in bare feet. The dress brushes her thighs, pools at her ankles. You try to sustain yourself as her, but even with your eyes closed you think: This isn't me. And then another voice says: This could have been me.

Out loud —I could have been a contender.

—What's that? Nancy asks, picking up the phone again.

—It's starting again, you say, and turn up the volume.

Dress #8

Your mother doesn't have anything suitable in her closet so the funeral director suggests you dress her in her everyday clothes. You tell him that for the last six months she wore her nightgown.

—That's unconventional, but not unheard of, he says.

—It's open casket.

—Lots of people are buried in their pajamas.

—Lots of people are assholes.

He clasps his hands loosely in front of him and respectfully says nothing.

You'd like to drive to the expensive department store downtown and buy her an evening gown, something outrageous with sequins, but you need to find something quickly. The funeral home needs an outfit by this evening. There is no time there is no time there is no time. Don't think. Go to Sears.

The stale perfume lingers from the scent counter. It's cold from too much air conditioning, but still, you sweat. Walk towards the sale rack where she always went. The dresses are leftovers from last season and heavy to the touch. They are wool, durable. Each is a dark wintry colour: dirt brown, slate grey, midnight blue and black, the obvious choice, the colour of oblivion. Pause on the black one, but fret over the size. Hear her saying "An extra large? I'm not that big." But worse, to buy it too small and have her flopping out of it. You figure the attendants can tuck it in if it's too big. It's marked down with overlapping red stickers, $145 to $99 to $75 to $49.

Cries erupt from your body. Heaving, terrible sounds. The Sears saleswoman brings you tissues and asks if she can help. Tell her that you can't pay $49 for the dress your mother will be buried in. You can't. You can't do that. She misunderstands and offers to ask her manager if she can get it further reduced. Explain that you want to pay the full price of the dress. This is important to you. You try not to cry on the dress but your tears, snot, and saliva create darker black spots on the material. At the cash, the saleswoman is unable to charge you anything but the reduced sale price. It's in the system, she tells you several times. Accept that you will bury your mother in the dress marked seventy-five percent off.

In her coffin she looks like a real estate agent. She fills the box as though her body is a batter poured into it. Part of you wants to crawl inside with her. Instead you stand next to her coffin like a protective guard. The funeral director plies you with coffee. Free refills. You spill it onto your shirt and half expect your mother to leap out of her coffin and blot it with a handkerchief. Even now she speaks to you. Welcome it. Rub your earlobe between your fingers and tilt your head as though you're enjoying a poignant memory. Then walk out to the parking lot and scream.

"A Meditation on Dresses" originally appeared in *PRISM International*.

Children of the New World

by Alexander Weinstein

Sometimes, when evening comes and the light hits our home in a way that reminds us of that other life, we'll talk about them. What their faces looked like, the feeling of their weight in our arms, the way our youngest would crawl onto my back. I'll see Mary sitting alone in our living room, the sun gone, just the reds of dusk outlining the trees, and I know she's remembering them. I walk over, put my arms around her, or kneel by her and place my head in her lap, and we'll stay like that, holding one another's pain, wondering whether we are truly monsters.

They weren't real, we say, looking for confirmation. Right?

Right.

Then we get up, start dinner, and move on with our childless lives.

*

For those of us who became parents in those first years, we remember the awe and beauty of that new world. To lie down in the darkness of the chamber, adjust the pillow beneath our heads, and log on was tantalizing. The chamber's darkness gave way to the light of the other world, the white walls of our online home appearing before us, filling our teeth with electric joy. We recall the first steps we took in our new house. To reach out and touch the world was to be illuminated, and we walked outside to see the homes lined up along our street shining and new, other users emerging from doorways, waving as they crossed their lawns to make introductions. Isn't this incredible? Where are you using from? Las Cruces, Copenhagen, Austin. We were like babies. Like Adam and Eve some said. We reached out towards one another to see how skin felt; we let our neighbors' hands run across our arms. In this world, we seemed to understand, we were free to experience a physical connection that we'd always longed for in the real world but had never been able to achieve. Who can blame us for being reckless?

Perhaps such thoughts seem childish now, in light of all that happened; yet it's often those first weeks of usage, when the world was still new, that Mary and I speak of most when we remind ourselves that life was good. It was just a beautiful illusion, we tell one another, a fantastic electronic diversion. Right? Right, we say.

*

Mary's pregnancy took us both by surprise. She had gone through menopause a decade earlier and we'd resigned ourselves to living childless lives. We'd waited too long, had debated the pros and cons too many times, had placed our jobs first, and then it was too late. It was only when Mary's belly began to swell that we accessed the FAQ tab. It was all there, no great mystery: pregnancy worked the same as in the real world, fully explained in the tutorial. We had planned to watch the walk-thru at some point, had gotten as far as the instruction to roll our thoughts to the left to select our tattoos and piercings, up and down for musculature and age, but then we began playing with landscapes and playlists, and before we knew it we had the basics of navigation down. This is how you upload music to the home speakers; this is how you project your photos onto the living room wall; this is how you place one hand on your wife's hips; this is how she puts her hand behind your neck; this is how you kiss. And then she was pregnant.

The FAQs informed us we could remove an unwanted pregnancy as easily as dragging a file to the recycle bin, but we were curious. Here would be a program, created entirely outside our control, another being formed from the combination of our genome preferences. The birth promised to be as quick and painless as a download. So we held each other, scrolled through online baby names, and agreed to bring new life into this world.

In this new world, Mary and I proved to be a completely different couple. Our bodies became freed from habit, independent of hormonal changes. We grew hungry for the electric hum of one another. Mary soon became pregnant again and our lives became illuminated in a way we'd thought impossible in the physical world. Online, with our new family, we had found joy.

*

June had just turned three, Oscar two, when Mary and I began to explore. By then most everyone had heard of the Dark City. It was there on the horizon, out over the tree line of our neighborhood, a brown glow in the distance. It was common knowledge you could travel to the city to spend a few hours, days even, among its pleasure domes and massage parlors. When I'd log off and go to work, the other men at the office made jokes about it, a delicious guilt within their laughter. Smoothest bodies you'll ever feel, they confided. It was said there were parlors where air currents tickled the body to the edge of orgasm. There were morphing temples where skin became ecstatic mounds of quivering Jell-O. We were intrigued. I'd go if you went, we agreed. So, one night late in January, after the children had fallen asleep, we left them with an online babysitter and headed for the Dark City

I'd once witnessed Amsterdam's Red Light district with its windows of naked bodies and its rotten maroon lights. I can still smell its cobblestones, thick with dirt, and see the doorways, dark with hungry faces. This was what I'd imagined The Dark City would resemble, and I'd expected to be repulsed when we approached its gates, to turn back with shame and relief, to write the place off as a tasteless distraction. But, though the city oozed a seedy brown light, up close the streets were lit by warm yellow lamps humming with electricity. The gates of its many entrances stood open, so welcoming that turning away was impossible. We saw men and women emerging from its depths, setting off into the sky to return home. There was no danger in exploring a block or two, we reasoned.

So we entered the first ring of the city, filled with its soft-core delights, its toy shops and kissing booths. The stores reflected the amber glow of lamps, which brightened the faces of other tourists who walked the streets: couples with their arms around one another, college kids sitting on curbs kissing, single men walking with their hands in their pockets. A Korean man by a foot massage parlor called out to us, "Beautiful Asian girls. Twenty credits for fifteen minutes." Across the street, a gorgeous man called my wife sweetie and invited us inside to be tickled. And rising above the lights and the busy streets, one could hear the collective moans from deep within the web of avenues, pulling us forward towards the core, where we longed to play.

The Air Current Hotels were four blocks in. White, three-story buildings with darkened windows and velvet ropes leading to their doors. At the check-in desk, a teenage receptionist in a string-top charged my account forty credits for the session.

"It's our first time."

"You'll love it!" she said. "You've never experienced air like this!" She smiled and directed us towards the elevators. "Second floor, room number seventeen."

"What do we do there?"

"Just close the door and stand in the middle of the room. We'll take it from there."

We rode the elevator to the second floor and found the room entirely empty, the lights dimmed. I shut the door behind us and we stepped into the middle of the room. A light draft played along the floor, working its way up my pant legs and finding the softness behind my knees. Another breeze caressed my neck then slid down my collar. Our feet were lifted from the ground and we floated horizontally, air currents tickling our skin with alternating nips of cold and warmth. Wind rubbed against my lips, playing against my tongue; a strong gust pushed against my chest, holding me down. I reached out to hold onto Mary, but there was nothing except air, and I was filled with the luxurious thought that I was being made love to by a goddess of wind. Mary arched her back, pushing down into the gusts which caressed her again and again, until her body was vibrating, peaked by wind, and we blossomed together, our bodies becoming one with the network of electrons buzzing around us.

In this way, Mary and I became one of the many couples walking with their arms around one another, post-orgasmic and giddy, on the streets of the Dark City. We graduated from the Air Current Hotels to the Thousand-Finger Parlors—where we lay with our eyes closed, holding one another's hands as invisible fingers rubbed us to climax—and later on to the second ring of the city, with its Morphing Temples. We explored our bodies as sea creatures and woodland animals. Mary would transform into a blue-eyed doe, and I, a buck, would brush my antlers against her fur as I mounted her. There was a beautiful playfulness to it all, and we rekindled our passion, which was restricted to our online lives. For when we returned to our chambers at home and changed out of our clothes, we did so with cybernetic exhaustion, barely noticing our naked bodies which brushed against one another in the bathroom. And when we kissed goodnight we didn't linger. This, however, seemed a small price to pay for our online pleasures, and if we felt disconnected from one another in the real world, we attempted to pay this little heed, focusing instead on that moment, every night, when our children were asleep and we'd set off to seek our individual pleasures together.

*

Mary found the man in our bathroom shortly after we'd visited the Bondage Cathedral. I heard her scream from the other side of the house. He stood there, his body flickering cheaply, a low resolution pale-faced man whose body pixilated in places. His erection, however, glowed in high resolution, and when he saw Mary he said, "I want to please you in sixty-nine ways," before she slammed the door shut and yelled for help. When I opened the door, the man was stroking himself, looking down at his enormous penis. "I can help you grow three inches naturally," he told me.

The FAQs didn't cover this. And it was only searching through other users' blogs that we figured out how to delete him from our home. But during our next session, when the doorbell rang, we opened the front door and encountered a man from Ghana who told us he was a distant relative. He'd brought our children presents, he said. He needed our credit number to upload the toys for the kids. We locked the door but we could see the man outside, pacing first on our porch, and then climbing into our bushes to knock on our windows. We deleted the African man, but when night came, our lamps no longer lit our home with soft warmth but contained a shadowy light, and our house was filled with the feeling of being watched by countless eyes, our every action scanned for information.

Mary took the children into our bedroom and I logged off to call online support. The man on the other end of the line spoke broken-English, the line buzzing from overseas connection. He tried a couple options with me, and finally said, "Sir, your account is corrupted. You will have to reset all files to the initial settings."

"What's that mean?"

"You must delete all data from your account—your preferences, photos and music. You will need to recreate your bodies again. I see you have children."

"Yes."

"You will need to delete them."

"*What?*"

"The virus has spread to them. You will have to delete them and begin again. I'm sorry, sir."

"*There's no way I'm deleting my children!*"

"Yes, sir, I understand. It is your choice. But the system has a fatal error; it will only get worse. You will not want your children in that house soon."

"Put your supervisor on."

"Yes, sir," the man said. Then I was put on hold for ten minutes of light jazz until a supervisor, and later her supervisor, told me the same information: that we should have installed an anti-virus protection plan. Without it, there was little left to do but return our system to factory settings.

"What if we move to a new house?"

"I'm afraid all of your family is corrupted," the supervisor told me. "You'll just end up bringing the virus with you. It's an easy process to reboot. Simply hold down the power button on your console for twenty seconds and—"

"*These are my children!*" I yelled.

"If it's any consolation, they won't feel a thing; they're just data."

I hung up the phone and told Mary the news. There was no way, we agreed, that we would reboot. We'd have to be vigilant, delete each and every file when they appeared. The kids could sleep in our room; we'd take shifts keeping watch over them. I called in sick to work and Mary used her vacation days, but within a week nowhere was safe. A bronze-skinned man with spikey hair appeared in our bedroom, telling Mary there were guys like him waiting to connect with her. A woman who looked like my mother transmogrified in the living room, saying she'd been robbed and needed our help to pay for groceries. We had to restrain our children from running to her when she called out their names. Toys began appearing around the house; to touch a single one was to transmit all of our information across an unsecure interface. We hid the children beneath blankets, telling them this was all a game we were playing. And then, one evening, we found ourselves surrounded, every room of the house filled with cartoon characters hawking downloadable games and attractive women selling vibrators and wrinkle cream.

"We don't have a choice," I finally said to Mary. "You can stay with them and hold them. I'll log out and do it."

"Do what, Daddy?" June asked, peeking out from the hut we'd built in the corner of our bedroom. We were silent for a moment.

"Nothing," I said quietly. "Come and give me a hug. You too, Oscar," I called, and our children emerged from the hut, climbing onto my lap to put their arms around me.

I often tell myself that I held them for as long as I could. It was worse for Mary; she felt their bodies disappear beneath her embrace.

*

Among my favorite memories: Snow. Its enhanced crystalline structure; its pristine whiteness; its silence. Oscar, June and I on a sled, zooming down a snowy hill which spools endlessly ahead of us. Oscar saying, "Make it steeper, Daddy," and June pointing at the corn-piped snowman bowing to us and tipping his top hat as we speed by. And when we walk back to the house, our sled dragging behind us, the quiet end of the day, dusk falling along the horizon, the snow lilac with evening.

Mary's favorite memory: A morning in spring, the soft light breaking through our windows and lighting up the wood floors. I'm playing with June, rolling a small Matchbox car back and forth, and Oscar is sleeping in her arms, our family together and quiet in the morning light.

Things I regret: raising my voice. The look of surprise those moments before hurt sets in. And for what? For taking too long putting on their shoes; for not wanting to sleep when I was ready to log off; for asking me to read another chapter; for being children. There's no way you can give everything to your children, no way you can spend every minute with them or be there for each hour of their lives. But give me a second chance and I'd never log off. I'd read them stories till they were deep asleep, hold them tightly though the darkness, and tell them I loved them once again. The feeling of parenthood never leaves you. Not when I go to work now. Not when Mary and I go to dinner or sit alone at the movie theater.

*

Every Sunday, Mary and I go to the support group they hold over in Corvallis at the community center. It's facilitated by Bill Thompson, a large, heavyset man with a salt and pepper beard who reminds us of a grizzly bear. He's a warm hearted guy, gruff in a comforting way, who smokes Marlboro Reds outside during breaks. Every meeting he brings a basket of assorted teas and coffee for us, arranges our chairs in a circle, and offers a hug more readily than a handshake. One of his common pieces of wisdom is, "Don't let anyone tell you they weren't real." He puts his fingers over his heart and taps softly. "They were real here." Of everyone who attends, he's undoubtedly lost the most; he had a family of five and a wife he'd met online who turned out to be a scammer. She'd taken it all from him: drained his savings, stolen his identity, and infected the children. Not that we should compare losses, he tells us. There's no hierarchy to pain. "Our work isn't to figure out who hurts the most," he says. "Our work is to heal."

We take turns. New members tell their stories first. They go through the stages many of us have gone through. They show us their photos—if they're lucky enough to have printed them—they talk about the smell of their children, the colors of the clothing they were wearing on the last day before they rebooted. They cry, and Bill holds the space for them, gives them a hug when it seems like they'll accept one, and teaches us how to grieve. "We all have to reboot *this*," he says and motions to the room with his open palms. "This world, with all its pain and loss. This is where we learn to love again."

Bill's been a real savior to Mary and me. For a long time there was no one to share our pain with. We have friends and they're good-hearted, well-meaning people, but they never had kids on the other side. They comfort us for a while, a couple weeks, a month; they send sympathy cards and flowers, but in the end they all offer the same advice: It's time to move on. They were just programs. You can create new children. And we nod grimly, knowing full well we'll never return.

Bill's advice has helped us get to a place where we can say what happened wasn't our fault, that we're not monsters, that our children didn't die because of us. We were lonely. We were needful. We wanted to feel pleasure again, to be caressed and loved. Our longings were those of humans, not monsters. No, the real monsters in this world are the hackers and scammers, faceless men and women who destroy lives for the joy of testing a virus, and who sacrificed our children to make a buck.

When the meetings are over, Bill invites us to be physical like we were in the other world. "Human contact is all there really is," he says. And so we put our arms around one another, timidly at first, and eventually with all the warmth of our bodies. We hold the others who come, the parents and widowers, the aunts, uncles, and grandparents. We pull strangers into our embrace and hold them tightly against us. There's nothing electronic about the gesture, no hum to the body, only the warmth of their breathing and the beating of their hearts.

"Children of the New World" originally appeared in *Pleiades* as recipient of the Gail-Crump Prize in Fiction.

Contributors

Allison Adair's most recent work appears in *Best New Poets 2015, Mississippi Review, Nimrod, Shenandoah, Southwest Review*, and *Tahoma Literary Review*. Winner of the Orlando Prize and the Fineline Competition, Adair teaches at Boston College and Grub Street.

Loren Bienvenu is a freelance arts and culture journalist and woodworker based in New Mexico.

Amy Bonnaffons is a writer living in Athens, GA. Her writing has appeared in *Kenyon Review, The Sun, The New York Times*, and elsewhere. She is currently working on a novel and a book of short stories. Amy is also a founding editor of *7x7.la*, a literary magazine publishing collaborative work between writers and visual artists.

Christie Chapman is a writer and editor in the Washington, DC area. Her short fiction and non-fiction have appeared in *The Moustache Club of America*, a microsite of *The Good*

Men Project, and *Penny & Farthing*. A former journalist, she is currently working on a book about that crazy time she got laid off and moved out West and spent her days of unemployment hanging out with homeless folks and people who lived on their boats.

Melanie Cheng's work has appeared in *Meanjin, Overland, Griffith Review, Sleepers Almanac, The Bridport Prize Anthology*, and elsewhere. Her short story collection, *Australia Day*, won the 2016 Victorian Premier's Literary Award for Unpublished Manuscript.

Kevin A. Couture's writing has appeared in *Beloit Fiction Journal, Kestrel, Grain, The Fiddlehead, The Antigonish Review, The Dalhousie Review, PRISM international, Event*, and others. He has been nominated for the Writers' Trust of Canada/McClelland & Stewart Journey Prize and was included in the anthology *Coming Attractions*. A collection of stories, *Lost Animal Club*, was released in September 2016 by NeWest Press.

Barbara Dahlberg is a retired art teacher living and working in Pittsburgh's Regent Square. Her work has appeared in the *Pittsburgh Post Gazette*, the *Pittsburgh City Paper*, and *U.S.1 Worksheets*. She is a fellow with the Western Pennsylvania Writing Project and a Carlow University Mad Woman in the Attic.

Hilary Dean was the winner of CBC's Canada Writes Non-fiction award in 2012, and has won *EVENT Magazine*'s Non-fiction contest twice. Her work has been named as a

Notable Essay in *Best American Essays 2015*, appeared in *This Magazine* and *Matrix,* and has shortlisted for the Journey Prize and HG Wells competition. Dean's recent film, *So You're Going Crazy...* currently airs on CBC's Documentary Channel. www.hilarydean.ca

Gay Degani's suspense novel *What Came Before* is available in trade paperback and e-book formats. She writes flash, short stories, and essays on the art and craft of writing. She blogs at "Words in Place," where a complete list of her published work can be found. She's had four stories nominated for Pushcart consideration and won the 11th Annual Glass Woman Prize.

Ryann Eastman is a California native and MFA candidate at Indiana University.

Jen Fawkes's work has appeared in *One Story, Crazyhorse, The Iowa Review,* Amazon's *Day One, Shenandoah, Michigan Quarterly Review,* and elsewhere. Her stories have won prizes from *Washington Square,* Writers @ Work, *Blue Earth Review,* and *Salamander.* She holds an MFA from Hollins University and a BA from Columbia University.

Pete Fromm's latest book is the memoir *The Names of the Stars.* He is a five time winner of the Pacific Northwest Booksellers Literary Award for his novels *If Not For This, As Cool As I Am,* and *How All This Started,* a story collection, *Dry Rain,* and the memoir, *Indian Creek Chronicles.* The film version of *As Cool As I Am,* starring Claire Danes, James Marsden, and Sarah Bolger, was released in 2013. He is the author of four other short story collections and has published over two hundred stories in magazines. He is on the faculty of Oregon's Pacific University's Low-Residency MFA Program.

Megan Gilmore currently lives in Chicago. Besides words, she enjoys theatre, photography, and cooking pasta.

Jennifer Givhan is an NEA fellow in poetry and the winner of the 2015 Pleiades Editors' Prize for her poetry collection *Landscape With Headless Mama*. A Mexican-American poet who grew up in the Imperial Valley, she was a PEN/Rosenthal Emerging Voices Fellow, a Pinch Poetry Prize winner, and a DASH Literary Journal Poetry Prize winner. She earned her MFA from Warren Wilson College. Her work has appeared in *Best New Poets 2013, AGNI, Southern Humanities Review, Prairie Schooner, Indiana Review, Rattle, The Collagist,* and *The Columbia Review.* She is assistant editor at *Tinderbox Poetry Journal* and she teaches composition and poetry at Western New Mexico University and The Rooster Moans Poetry Coop.

Don Hogle is a poet, blogger and brand and communications strategist living in Manhattan. *Mud Season Review, Minetta Review, Blast Furnace, Shooter, DoveTales, Outrider Review, Clapboard House* and *Dirty Chai* are among the journals that have recently published his poetry. His website is donhoglepoet.com.

Matt Hohner, a Baltimore native, holds an MFA in Writing and Poetics from Naropa University in Boulder, Colorado.

His work has recently been a finalist for the Ballymaloe International Poetry Prize, and taken both third and first prizes in the Maryland Writers Association Poetry Prize. His work has appeared recently in *The Moth*, *The Irish Times*, *Free State Review*, and *The Sow's Ear*.

Robin Hunter's first short screenplay, "The Night," was produced in 2012 and has currently been accepted for screening at three film festivals. "Lazy Lies" is her first published work of fiction.

Jeanne Julian's poems have appeared in *Naugatuck River Review* and other journals, also winning awards in competitions sponsored by *The Comstock Review*, The North Carolina Poetry Society, The Lanier Library, and the Asheville Writers' Workshop. Former editor of a photography newsletter, she was the featured photographer in *moonShine review*, Summer 2015. Her chapbook, *Blossom and Loss*, was published by Longleaf Press in 2015.

David Karosick holds a degree in Literature from Georgia State University. His fiction appears in *Whiskey Island* and *Sakura Review* and has been shortlisted for the Bridport Prize. He lives with his family in the East Bay.

Scott Kauffman's most recent novel is *Revenants—The Odyssey Home*, published by Moonshine Cove Publishing. He is the recipient of the 2010 Hackney Literary Award and the 2011 Mighty River Short Story Contest prize.

Aimee LaBrie works as a communications director at Rutgers University. Her short story collection, *Wonderful Girl*, was chosen for the Katherine Anne Porter Prize in Fiction and published by the University of North Texas Press in 2007. Her short stories have been published in *Pleiades, Minnesota Review, Iron Horse Literary Review, Permafrost*, and other literary journals. In 2012 she won first place in Zoetrope's All-Story Fiction contest and was also a finalist for a Pushcart Prize. Her second collection of short stories, *Animal Shelters*, was a finalist in the BOA Prize in Fiction in 2014. You can read her blog at butcallmebetsy.blogspot.com.

Scott Lambridis's debut novel, *The Many Raymond Days*, received the 2012 Dana Award. His stories have appeared in *Slice, Memorious, Cafe Irreal, Flash Fiction Funny, New American Writing*, and other journals. He recently completed his MFA from San Francisco State where he received the Miriam Ylvisaker Fellowship and three literary awards. Before that, he earned a degree in neurobiology, and co-founded Omnibucket.com, through which he co-hosts the Action Fiction! performance series.

Marjorie Maddox is Sage Graduate Fellow of Cornell University (MFA) and Professor of English and Creative Writing at Lock Haven University. She has published 11 collections of poetry, most recently *True, False, None of the Above* from the Poiema Poetry Series; the short story collection *What She Was Saying* (Fomite Press); and over 500 poems, stories, and essays in journals and anthologies. For more information, please see www.marjoriemaddox.com

Previously unpublished, Cassidy McCants has received two honorable mentions from Glimmer Train. She lives in Tulsa, Oklahoma and is associate editor of *Nimrod International Journal* at The University of Tulsa. She is currently an MFA student in fiction at Vermont College of Fine Arts.

Randi Miller's fiction has been published in *Dogwood: A Journal of Poetry and Prose*, has been a finalist in *Glimmer Train's* New Writer's Contest 2015, has been nominated for UCLA's Kirkwood Award, and received honorable mention at the Santa Barbara Writer's Conference.

Eric Nelson's most recent collection, *Some Wonder*, published by Gival Press as the winner of the 2014 Gival Press Poetry Award, is his sixth book of poetry. He lives in Asheville, NC.

"A Choice of Words" originally appeared in Valerie Nieman's second poetry collection, *Hotel Worthy,* published in 2015. She has held an NEA creative writing fellowship as well as state grants in West Virginia and North Carolina. She is the author of the novels *Blood Clay*, honored with the Eric Hoffer Prize in General Fiction, *Survivors*, and *Neena Gathering*, and a collection of short stories, *Fidelities*. Her awards include the Greg Grummer, Nazim Hikmet, and Byron Herbert Reece poetry prizes. A former newspaper reporter and editor, she teaches creative writing at North Carolina A&T State University and was a founding editor of both *Kestrel* and *Prime Number* magazines.

A graduate of Eastern Washington University, Neleigh Olson is an actor, writer, artist and Thoroughbred exercise rider currently enrolled in the University of Kentucky's creative writing MFA program.

Melissa Ostrom lives in rural western New York with her husband and children. She serves as a public school curriculum consultant, teaches English at Genesee Community College, and writes whenever and however much her four-year-old and six-year-old let her. Her fiction has appeared in *Monkeybicycle*, *decomP*, *Oblong*, *Cleaver*, *Flash*, and elsewhere.

Michael Pearce's poems and stories have appeared in *Epoch*, *The Gettysburg Review*, *The Yale Review*, *Poems & Plays*, *Nimrod*, *Conjunctions*, *Witness*, and elsewhere. He lives in Oakland, California, and plays saxophone in the Bay Area band Highwater Blues.

Brenda Peynado's stories have been selected for the *O. Henry Prize Stories 2015* and received prizes from the Chicago Tribune's Nelson Algren Award, Writers at Work and the *Glimmer Train* Fiction Open Contest. Her work appears or is forthcoming in *The Threepenny Review*, *Epoch*, *Shenandoah*, *Mid-American Review*, *Black Warrior Review*, *Pleiades*, *Colorado Review*, *Cimarron Review*, and others. She received her MFA from Florida State University and is currently a PhD student at the University of Cincinnati.

Mark Ramirez is from Toledo, Ohio. His work has appeared or is forthcoming in *San Pedro River Review*, *The*

Lascaux Review, and *Great Lakes Review.* He is an MFA student at the University of Alabama.

Brittney Scott's first poetry collection, *The Derelict Daughter,* won the 2015 New American Poetry Prize. She is also a recipient of the Joy Harjo Prize for Poetry, as well as the Dorothy Sargent Rosenberg Poetry Prize. Her poems have appeared in *Best New Poets, Prairie Schooner, The New Republic, Narrative Magazine, Cincinnati Review, Alaska Quarterly Review, Linebreak, Indiana Review* and elsewhere. She homesteads on seven acres in rural Virginia.

Karen Smyte, the founder of Red Beard Press, a youth-driven publishing press based out of Ann Arbor's teen center, The Neutral Zone, is the recipient of Mesa Refuge and Vermont Studio Residencies, as well as a 2016 Barbara Deming Memorial Grant. Chapters from her current novel-in-progress have been performed at Selected Shorts at Symphony Space and awarded 2nd place in the Bridport Prize. A former Canadian national team rower, newspaper reporter, and collegiate rowing coach, she now serves as President of Children's Literacy Network and records incarcerated mothers and grandmothers reading bedtime stories to their children.

Chelsea Sutton is a 2016 PEN Center USA Emerging Voices Fellow. Her fiction has appeared in *Spectrum, Bourbon Penn, The Texas Observer,* and others. Her plays have been developed in Los Angeles, Santa Barbara, Houston and New York. She is currently working on a collection of short stories called *Curious Monsters.*

Bob Thurber is the author of *Paperboy: A Dysfunctional Novel* and two collections of short fiction. His work has appeared in *Esquire* and many other publications as well as more than 40 anthologies. He is the recipient of The Marjory Bartlett Sanger Award, The Meridian Editors' Prize, and The Barry Hannah Fiction Prize.

Marcia Walker's fiction has been published in *Room*, *Prism international*, *University of Toronto Magazine*, and *The Broken Social Scene Story Project* (House of Anansi Press). Her creative nonfiction has appeared in magazines and journals in Canada and the US, including *The Globe and Mail* and on CBC radio. She's currently an MFA student at Guelph University.

Alexander Weinstein is the director of The Martha's Vineyard Institute of Creative Writing. He is the author of the collection *Children of the New World* (Picador 2016) and his short stories and translations have appeared in *Cream City Review*, *Notre-Dame Review*, *Pleiades*, *PRISM International*, *Rio Grande Review*, *Salamander*, *Sou'Wester*, *World Literature Today*, and other journals. He is the recipient of a Sustainable Arts Foundation Award, and his fiction has been awarded the Lamar York, Gail Crump, and New Millennium Prize.

Luke Wortley lives in Indianapolis, where he teaches Spanish at an inner-city school. He is the Co-founder and Editor-in-Chief of *Axolotl*, an online and print journal of weird, literary fibers. His work has appeared or is forth-coming in *Inch*, *Pea River Journal*, and *Milkfist*.

Ruth Wyer's stories have appeared in *Sleepers*, *Spineless Wonders*, *The Canary Press*, and have been broadcast on ABC Radio National. She is a winner of the Zinewest and the Margaret River Short Story Competitions.

Elaine Zimmerman is a policy leader for children, essayist, and poet. Her poetry has appeared in *Americana*, *Coal Hill Review*, *Lilith*, *Adanna Literary Journal*, *Winning Writers*, and elsewhere, and in anthologies including *Everybody Says Hello*, *Sleeping with One Eye Open*, *Encore*, *Inner Landscapes*, *Writers Respond to the Art of Virginia Dehn*, and *Worlds in Our Words: Contemporary American Women Writers*. Recent honors include the William Stafford, Al Savard and Morton and Elsie Prouty Memorial Awards.

www.ingramcontent.com/pod-product-compliance
Lightning Source LLC
Chambersburg PA
CBHW022158260626
47155CB00019B/3087